OTHER YEARLING BOOKS YOU WILL ENJOY:

YEARLING BOOKS are designed especially to entertain and enlighten young people. Patricia Reilly Giff, consultant to this series, received her bachelor's degree from Marymount College and a master's degree in history from St. John's University. She holds a Professional Diploma in Reading and a Doctorate of Humane Letters from Hofstra University. She was a teacher and reading consultant for many years, and is the author of numerous books for young readers.

For a complete listing of all Yearling titles, write to
Dell Readers Service,
P.O. Box 1045,
South Holland, IL 60473.

Under the Blood-Red Sun

GRAHAM SALISBURY

A Yearling Book

·Published by
Bantam Doubleday Dell Books for Young Readers
a division of
Bantam Doubleday Dell Publishing Group, Inc.
1540 Broadway
New York, New York 10036

ISBN: 0-440-41139-4

Reprinted by arrangement with Delacorte Press

Printed in the United States of America

December 1995

10   9   8   7   6   5   4   3   2   1   OPM

In Memory of
Henry Forester Graham, USN
Guy Fremont Salisbury, USN

And in Honor of
the Men of the 100th Infantry Battalion
and the 442nd Regimental Combat Team
of World War II,
United States Army

Mahalo nui loa to
Lani Teshima-Miller, Hank Arita,
Thurston and David Twigg-Smith,
the news library of *The Honolulu Advertiser*
and *The Honolulu Star-Bulletin*,
and the University of Hawai'i and Hawaii State
Library Hawaiiana collections.

Under the Blood-Red Sun

1

The Flag

It all started the day Grampa Joji decided to wash his precious flag of Japan and hang it out on the clothesline for the whole world to see. It was almost as big as the canvas tarp Papa used on his boat when it rained.

It was early September, 1941, just three weeks before the Yankees and the Dodgers started the World Series. A Sunday. Mama's day off. No breeze. The clouds, like giant white coral heads, hovered out over the ocean far beyond Honolulu harbor. In that kind of weather you stayed in the shade, at least if you were as smart as my dog Lucky, who lounged in the cool, weedless dirt under the house.

But anyway, Grampa scrubbed that flag clean. Usually, my friend Billy Davis and I thought it was pretty funny when he did something strange like that—like wash a flag, or take a bath in the stream, or laugh hysterically at Laurel and Hardy movies. Once, we got thrown out of a theater because Grampa kept on laughing, laughing, laughing, even when everyone else was quiet. Billy and I were nearly crying, Grampa was so funny. Grampa got mad and chased us. He was pretty tough about showing respect for your elders.

But a Japanese flag hanging out in the open like that was nothing to laugh about.

"Hey, Grampa," I yelled as I came up the dirt path through the trees. "Take that thing down. What if somebody _sees_ it?"

Billy was with me. We'd just gotten off the bus from a trip downtown to play baseball. I threw my catcher's mitt on the ground and started walking faster. Grampa stood in front of his flag like a fisherman showing off a big one.

The white flag had a red ball in the center, with red rays like searchlights shooting out from it. Grampa waved his hand toward the clothesline. "Hey, busta, good, nah? Confonnit!"

"No! Not good! How many times do we have to tell you? This place is American, not Japanese. _American._ Didn't you hear what Papa said? Too many Japanese around here, that's what a lot of people think. . . . They don't need to see that flag to remind them."

I brushed past him and pulled the wet flag down. It soaked my shirt. Grampa's eyes got big, like he was so surprised he didn't know what to do.

"Papa's worried enough about what the Hawaiians think of us, and what the _haoles_ think of us," I said. "We don't need anyone to think we're anti-_American_ too. There's a war going on, you know. And Japan isn't making any friends around here. Papa told you that already. Don't you remember?"

Grampa narrowed his eyes and clenched his fists. His face turned red and his lips bridged into a fish-scowl. "You Japanee!" he said. "Japanee!"

"American," I said. I took a step back and shoved the flag up onto the porch. "No good, Grampa. No good at *all!*"

Grampa's face grew redder. He shook his fist at me. "Whatchoo think you? You Japanee. Japanee inside. Like me, like Papa."

"Criminy," I said, walking a wide path around him. "This isn't Wakayama, you know. This isn't Japan. This is America, and you're going to get us in a lot of trouble with that stupid flag."

Just then Mama came out of the house. She didn't look too happy to be bothered on her only day off, the day she used to mend everybody's clothes. *"Nani-yo?* Whassamatta out here, Tomi? What you doing?"

"Grampa got the flag out again."

"Ojii-chan. He is *ojii-chan."*

"Same thing," I mumbled.

Mama frowned at me, then at Grampa. My little sister, Kimi, peeked around Mama's apron, then inched back out of sight when she saw Billy. She was afraid of him because he was so tall. He was only thirteen, like me, but almost a head taller. And he was white, a *haole.* But most of all, Billy was *kimpatsu*—with yellow hair. Grampa said in Japan it was a freak of nature to have yellow hair, but I never told Billy that.

In Japanese, Mama said, "Can't you listen to your

grandson, *ojii-chan*?" Then in English, "Mr. Wilson no like that kine . . . we could lose this house!"

Grampa started to say something to her in Japanese, which he always went back to when he was too mad to think.

"English," Mama said.

Grampa squinted at Mama. English was okay for me and Kimi, but for him it was no fun. He tried to learn it by listening to the police on the radio, but still wasn't picking it up very well. Poor Grampa. I felt sorry for him sometimes. But Papa said, "Too many people worried about Japanee . . . speak Ing-lish," or "Speak 'merican." Lucky for me, because my Japanese was about as good as Grampa's English.

Mama and Grampa glared at each other.

It drove Grampa crazy that Mama was so stubborn. He was always telling Papa he should teach her more respect. "She shame you," Grampa said. "She shame the family." But Papa just let Mama be herself.

She wagged a finger at Grampa. "You don't fool me. . . . I know you understand." Mama dragged up the sopping, crumpled flag, and went on with her warning in Japanese.

"Confonnit," Grampa said. *"Kuso."*

"Ooo, Grampa," I said. "No need to talk nasty."

Mama shook her head. Then she noticed Billy and nodded. "Billy-kun."

"Hi, Mrs. Nakaji," Billy said, then looked down and punched his baseball mitt.

Mama hauled the flag into the house with Kimi sticking to her apron like a tick.

Grampa started over to me. His long-sleeved khaki shirt, buttoned to the neck, and his wrinkled khaki pants made him look like he was one of those Pearl Harbor navy officers. His eyes said he wanted to wring my neck.

I backed away, and started running. Billy sprinted past me, heading through the trees toward the field where Papa kept his pigeons.

Ever since Grampa had to stop fishing with Papa because of a stroke, he'd been as snappy as a grouchy old dog. But his stroke didn't cripple him one bit. He followed us, walking at first, then faster. I ran past Billy, who laughed and tried to grab my shirt. "You coward," he said.

But Grampa went back to the house.

Luckily for Papa he was out fishing and wasn't due back for two more days. But Grampa would tell him, all right, and the story would be much bigger by then.

"He's so *dumb,* sometimes," I said.

"What would he have done if he'd caught you?" Billy asked, the two of us now down to a walk.

"Probably crack my head. Who knows with him?" Who could tell what he was thinking about anymore? Hanging his flag on the clothesline was as good as flying it from a pole.

Grampa knew Papa was worried. But then, Grampa was *issei,* first-generation Japanese immigrant, and looked at things in a certain way. The Japanese way—which was stern and obedient. He just wanted to work, and be honest. Like he did in Japan, where he was a fisherman. Nobody ever bothered anybody else. If somebody over there accidentally hurt somebody else, they'd make up for it, no matter how long it took. And if they died before they made up for it, then their descendants would take over. Grampa wanted me to think like that, he wanted Papa to beat me into "a boy of suitable devotion." Sometimes I thought he had a point. The old way was fair and honorable, which was good. But it was so inflexible. Jeese. Who knew *what* to think?

Billy and I both looked behind us at the same time, just to be sure Grampa was really gone. My house stood silently peeking back at me through the trees, a square box painted dark green. It sat on stilt-legs, about four feet off the ground—stilts to keep the rats and bugs out. It was the only home I'd ever known, and I loved it. I loved its silver-painted corrugated iron roof, which slanted down into gutters that flowed into the round water tank in the back. It made nice sounds in the rain. The only water we had was what we caught off the roof. Not like Billy's house, where they had water pipes from the street, and a bathroom inside the house.

"Hey," Billy whispered, quickly moving off the trail into the trees. His blond hair glowed where the sun hit it, but mostly he was in the shade. I crept up behind him and looked out through the trees at the grassy field.

Billy's brother, Jake.

And with him, Keet Wilson, the crazy boy, peeking into one of Papa's pigeon lofts with a stick in his hand.

Crazy Boy

Keet slapped the side of one of Papa's lofts with the stick. He laughed at the racket the birds made inside. I think he knew we were watching him.

Heat rushed over my skin in an angry wave. The only rest Papa ever got was when he spent time with his pigeons. And I was the one he trusted to take care of them when he was out working on the boat.

If Keet hurt those birds . . .

My hands started to shake. I wanted to punch him in the face.

No! Don't think like that! *Don't disgrace us,* Papa said. I could hear him as if he were standing next to me. *Don't cause trouble and bring shame to the Nakaji name again!* Papa was so worried about losing face.

Keet scraped the side of the loft with the stick, then stuck the point through the chicken-wire door and twirled it around. My jaw hurt, I was clamping my teeth so hard. Even Papa's warning couldn't keep me from feeling like fighting, sometimes. I didn't care if Mama *was* the Wilsons' maid.

"He knows we're watching him," I said.

Billy frowned. "Come on, let's get out of here."

"No. I can't just let him do that."

I took a deep breath and started out into the sunlight. One thing was sure—if Keet Wilson wanted to go crazy, no one could stop him, not even Billy's brother, who was bigger than all of us. When Keet got mad, he couldn't even stop himself. Not until somebody got hurt.

"Well, if it isn't your punk brother and the fish boy," Keet said to Jake as we got closer. "Hey, Toe-mee-*ka*-zoo, your birds are bored. They need a little excitement."

That is the one thing I cannot accept from you. . . .

I stood next to Billy, who was tall enough to look directly into Keet's eyes. Jake waited off to the side, watching. He never said much to anyone. As far as I could tell, Jake was the only friend Keet had. Billy said Jake only did things with him because there was no one else around.

Keet stared at me and tapped the loft again. A curtain of brown hair hung over his left eye. Two fake army dog tags hung out of his shirt on a silver chain. He liked to brag that they were real, but I knew from Billy that Keet's father had them made up as a birthday present.

"Please," I said. "Don't . . . you'll scare them."

Keet hit the side of the loft harder—*Whack! Whack! Whack!*

The pigeons went wild, crying out, flapping their

wings. I wanted to pound Keet into the dirt. *If you are troublemaker, then I am troublemaker . . . I am bad father, bad family. I no teach you to fight in the dirt like dogs!* If I tangled with Keet, Papa said, Mr. Wilson would fire Mama and kick all of us off his land.

"Cut it out, Keet," Billy finally said.

Keet smiled, and poked Billy in the shoulder with the point of the stick. "Hey, Jake . . . maybe your stupid little brother didn't see what we saw."

Jake frowned at Billy.

Whack! Keet hit the loft again.

This time Billy threw down his mitt and tried to grab Keet's arm.

Keet dropped the stick and slammed Billy in the chest with the palms of his hands. Billy went flying to the ground. Under the short grass the sun-baked earth was as hard as cement. Billy's breath exploded out of him.

Jake grabbed Keet from behind. "That's enough."

Keet shoved him off, crazy-eyed, ready to fight even his friend. Billy tried to stand, but couldn't. He fell over, then rolled around with wide, terrified eyes, his mouth half open, trying to breathe. Jake bent over him and sat him up, then slapped his back.

I stood frozen, watching Billy. Tears filled the edges of his eyes. Breathe, Billy . . . *breathe!*

At last Billy started gulping in big breaths, like he was sobbing. The tears rolled down his face. He wiped them away, then bent over on his knees. After a minute or so he stood, slowly, not looking at anyone.

Keet put his face an inch from mine. I saw small red lines on his eyeballs. "You think I'm *stupid,* fish boy? You think I don't know what goes on around here?" A speck of spit hit my lip when he said *stupid*. "What are you flying that Jap flag over at your house for?"

I stared at him without answering.

He shoved me, and I fell back a step. "Maybe I'll tell my father about it," Keet said, suddenly fake-nice. "How about that?"

"No," I said. "No . . . it won't happen again. . . . I promise, it won't."

Keet smiled. He tapped the side of my face with his fingertips. "Good boy," he said, pausing to study me. Then he added, "I'll be watching."

Humiliation swelled in my throat. I squeezed my fists.

Keet shoved me away and opened the loft door. He whacked the stick around inside, hitting the walls and the pigeons. You could hear the birds banging around, running into each other. Keet finally pulled the stick out.

One by one the pigeons burst through the door and swooped up, dipping and rising, filling the clearing above the field. All seventeen of Papa's racers disappeared over the trees in less than a minute.

"There," Keet said, watching the last bird vanish. "That's what they needed."

"Billy," he said. "Come here."

Billy didn't move. Keet glared bloody swords at him. Slowly, Billy walked over.

Keet put his arm on Billy's shoulder. "Listen . . . I want you to stop hanging around with this Jap. It's disgusting to see you two acting like friends. . . . It makes me *sick*."

Billy stared at the ground. Keet grabbed his jaw and squeezed his mouth. "You hear me?"

Billy rolled his eyes over toward Jake.

Keet jerked his head back so Billy's eyes were level with his own. "You better think long and hard about where you stand, little punk."

"Let's go," Jake said.

Keet let go of Billy. Blurry red marks swelled on Billy's cheeks.

Jake grabbed Keet's arm. "Come on, let's get out of here."

Keet looked at the hand on his arm, then glared up at Jake.

Jake blinked, and let go. "Come on," he said, barely whispering.

Keet kept glaring, then turned away and spit.

The two of them slouched off into the trees like a couple of cocky sailors down on Hotel Street.

"Hana-kuso," I whispered. I punched my fist and went over to check the loft. The wire on the door was bent. It could have been worse. Keet could have knocked the loft off its legs. I put fresh grit and feed into the feeder and whispered calming sounds to the nervous pigeons in the other loft.

No birds anywhere; not even doves or mynah birds specked the light blue afternoon sky. The pigeons were long gone, probably racing out over the sea by now. But they'd be back.

I went out into the middle of the field where the sun swarmed around in the grass, my anger now melting down into a small, private shame.

It was quiet with only me and Billy there. Just the muffled hiss of the small irrigation stream that ran between Billy's house and mine. I lay down in the grass and gazed up at the sky. What was I going to say to Papa if Keet did tell his father about the flag? He could tell the story any way he wanted to. He could even say he asked me nicely to take it down and that I refused.

It was hard for me to believe that Keet and I were once pretty good friends.

I was about nine at the time, and Keet was eleven or twelve, back before Billy moved here from the mainland. I used to follow Keet around because he was older and knew a lot of things I didn't. Like how to call his dog with a whistle you couldn't even hear, or how to shoot a BB gun. And Keet was the one who introduced me to baseball. He even gave me one of his mitts so we could throw to each other, the same mitt I still used. Keet's name was written on it in fading black ink that I couldn't rub off.

Anyway, for a long time I used to go over to see him, until one day he started getting busy. I went again and again and he was never there. His mother would say things like "Keet can't play today," or "Keet is with his father," or "Keet isn't home."

But one day Keet answered the door himself. I'd found a half-rusted pocketknife in the jungle and wanted to show it to him.

"Come play," I said.

"No."

"What?"

"I said no. I don't want to play with you anymore."

"Why?" I asked.

He shrugged. "Just don't."

I remember standing there on his porch. I didn't know if I should leave, or what.

"Beat it," he said.

"What?" I couldn't believe he'd said that to me.

"Beat it."

I pulled the knife out and handed it to him. "Look what I found."

Keet took it, studied it. "Where'd you get it?"

"Found it in the jungle."

"It's mine."

"No, it's not. I found it." I tried to take it back, but he shoved me, and I fell. My arm hit the floor and stung like a hammer had hit it. "It's *mine,*" I said, holding my arm and struggling back up.

"Beat it, I said."

I charged him, and we got into a fight, right on the Wilsons' front porch.

That night Papa asked me about my bruises and scratches. He listened without blinking an eye, the muscles in his jaw working, tightening.

Then he told Mama and Kimi to leave the room.

"I work hard to have good life, good family," Papa said, drilling me with his eyes.

I looked down at my scratched hands and the yellow bruise that blotched part of my arm. Grampa stood by the screen door, listening.

"You disgrace me," Papa went on. "You fight and everyone think you troublemaker!" He bolted up, his chair tumbling back on the floor. I froze. I didn't know if he was going to slap me or what. He took a deep breath, then said in Japanese, "Tomikazu, we are Americans, it is true . . . but inside we are also Japanese. I don't care how angry you get, you cannot fight. You must learn *gamman*—patience. You cannot be a troublemaker and bring shame on this family."

He stared into my eyes a moment longer. "You have disgraced us, Tomikazu. That is the one thing I cannot accept from you. Go to your room," he said. "Go!"

Later that night, after Papa had gone to sleep, Mama called me out onto the porch. She brought me a small piece of candy and told me to sit on the steps, then sat next to me. "Papa angry because he no want you to bring shame on family . . . but Papa care about you, Tomi-kun."

"I know, Mama. It was all my fault."

Mama nodded. "That Wilson boy, he made you pretty mad?"

I peeked over at her and nodded.

She nodded back. "I know how that can be."

Silence.

Then, without looking at me, she said, "What you think of that boy?"

I hate his stupid guts, I wanted to say. *He's a jerk.*

I shrugged.

"What you think when you hear that name, Wilson?"

"I don't know," I mumbled.

"Think about how you feel when you hear that name, Keet Wilson."

He's a punk and a creep and I hate his guts was all I could come up with. I didn't want to be anywhere near him anymore.

Mama stood and looked up at the moon, arching her back. "You thinking you don't like that name right now. How come you think that?"

Because he's stupid, that's why. He stole my knife and pushed me into a fight.

I got up and stood next to her.

When I didn't say anything, Mama said, "Hoo, tired already. I going sleep. How's about you?"

I nodded and followed her back into the house. The rusty screen door hinges screeched in the stillness. I made sure it didn't slap when I closed it.

"One more thing, Tomi-kun. Whatever you think about that boy—do you want people to get that same thing in their minds when they think of Tomikazu Nakaji?"

Mama peeked into my eyes, then turned away, a look that said our confusing conversation was meant to tell me something important.

"Nakaji," Mama said, "must always be a *good* name."

Grampa was asleep on his mat. He'd left the candle burning for me. I pinched it out and eased down on my squeaky bed. I lay in the dark for a long, long time, thinking about the damage I had done.

• • •

Even now, in the warm, grassy field with Billy, I could still feel Mama's soft hand on my neck.

I shook the memory away. I could hear Lucky barking at something.

Billy came over and sat down next to me. "What's *hana-kuso* mean?"

"*Hana-kuso?*"

"That's what you called Keet after he left."

"I did?"

Billy nodded, and I smiled, remembering. "It means 'booger.'"

Billy laughed and shook his head. "You got that right."

"Hey, thanks for what you did," I said.

He nodded and held his glove under his nose, smelling the leather.

"Billy . . . what did Keet mean about *where you stand?*"

Billy bunched up his lips and shrugged. He dropped his glove and tore a blade of grass into tiny pieces, then tossed them away.

3

Mose and Rico

Mose and Rico Corteles were lounging on the grass like a couple of lizards when Billy and I pulled up in front of the school in Mr. Davis's shiny blue four-door Ford. My family didn't have a car, just Grampa's old bike. So it was lucky I could catch a ride with Billy. Otherwise it was the bus or a two-mile walk.

But this was the last year of that. Next year, in the ninth grade, Mr. Davis wanted Billy to go to Punahou, the *haole* private school—the white school. Keet Wilson and Jake already went there. Billy was supposed to start this year, but he fought like crazy to get out of it. So he got to stay one more year with us at Roosevelt.

Actually, what Billy really wanted to do was go to McKinley, a high school the *haoles* called Tokyo High because they had so many Japanese. They also had a first-rate baseball team, the Mick Sluggers. Billy went to all their games.

Our school didn't even have a baseball team, so Billy and I got together with a bunch of friends and played on our own. Most of the time we played against two other homemade teams, the Kaka'ako Boys and another team called the RBIs. We called ourselves the Rats. Rico made that up.

Billy's one big dream was to pitch in the majors—he wanted to be on the New York Yankees. He figured he could get good enough someday, and so did the rest of us. He could pitch like the Yankees' Red Ruffing, almost, or like Whit Wyatt on the Brooklyn Dodgers.

Anyway, there was Rico the lizard in front of the school, and Mose, dozing in the sun next to him.

Rico, who was Portuguese and played first base on the Rats, was Mose's cousin. He sat cross-legged with his elbows on his knees, chewing on a wooden match. He always had some of those in his pocket, even though he didn't smoke.

Mose was stretched out, propped up on his elbow. He played center field, which fit, because he was pretty quiet and liked to keep to himself.

The two of them looked like lazy bums, or else troublemakers. But they were pretty smart, and worked hard in school, except, of course, in Mr. Ramos's class, because Mr. Ramos was an easy teacher. He was also their uncle.

Mose and Rico liked to show off and look tough. Rico had a scar on his chin from when he went downtown with his father. A year ago Mr. Corteles had taken Rico and

Rico's sixteen-year-old cousin, Esther, downtown to pick up Esther's mother. Mr. Ramos was with them.

Anyway, while they were waiting around for Esther's mother to get off work, six drunk army guys came up and tried to drag Esther off with them. Esther screamed and Mr. Corteles grabbed one of the men. Mr. Ramos and Rico jumped into it, too, trying to push and shove the army guys away. One army guy slugged Rico and sent him flying into the gutter, where he hit his chin. Rico said the guy then went after Mr. Ramos.

Mr. Corteles managed to free Esther, but by the time the police got there, the army guys had already pounded him. Rico's chin was cut and bloody, and Mr. Ramos had a broken knuckle on his punching hand.

Now Rico hated the army, but he liked the scar. It looked good on him, and he told everyone he got it in a gang fight. Except, of course, when Mr. Ramos was within hearing distance.

Mose was an easygoing guy, but he could look mean if he wanted to. He always rolled the sleeves of his shirt up to show off his muscles.

But the thing about Mose and Rico, and Billy, too, was that they would stand by you no matter what. That was what the Rats were all about. Those guys were like brothers.

Rico pointed his gangster chin toward me and Billy as we walked up to them. "Heyyy," he said. Billy walked kind of stiff because of how he fell when Keet had pushed him.

"How much you and *haole* boy pay that chauffeur to

drive you in that limo-zeen?" Rico said, tipping his head toward Mr. Davis's car as it drove away.

"For me to know and you to find out," I said. "What? You jealous?"

"Shhh," Rico said with a lemon-sour look on his face.

"Hey—us two is hot shots," I said. "We pay good money for that chauffeur."

"What you two is, is dingdongs."

The bell rang, but we took our time shuffling into school. Mose, I noticed, had a small paper lunch bag, which seemed funny because we always ate cafeteria food.

Mose walked over to Billy and put his arm on his shoulder. "How'zit, *haole* boy?"

"Not bad," Billy answered. Billy didn't seem to mind being called *white boy* all the time. He always had a shy grin when you said it. Anyway, even if he did mind, he would never tell you to knock it off.

"Your daddy's car pretty sharp," Mose said. "I like that shiny paint. You never said your daddy was rich."

"Naw . . . he's not rich."

"Sheee, all *haoles* are rich."

Billy looked over at him, not knowing what to say. Billy was so easy to tease sometimes—so serious about everything.

Mose raised an eyebrow and nudged Billy. "That's all right. You can be rich . . . so long as you buy us all one soda pop after school, yeah?"

"Sure," Billy said.

"Naah," Mose said, cracking a smile. "Come on, I only joking. Hey, I got something for you." He pulled a brand-new baseball out of the paper bag. "Me and Rico wanted to give you this because you beat the Kaka'ako Boys for us. That felt good, man, really good."

The Kaka'ako Boys were a bunch of too-young-for-varsity baseball fanatics like us, stink-eyed mitt-punchers who were getting ready to play for the Mick Sluggers at McKinley. They were also pretty tough guys. On the Rats, I was the only Japanese, but the Kaka'ako Boys were *all* Japanese. They lived down by Queen Street, near the ocean, and some of them were from fishing families, which is how I got to know them. Mose and Rico could think of nothing better than to wipe the bases with Kaka'ako baseball caps.

Billy's eyes widened. He took the ball from Mose and rubbed it in both hands, like he was working it down, getting it ready. You could tell Mose had choked him up. "Thanks . . ." Billy said to Mose and Rico. "I . . . it's a nice ball . . . thanks."

Rico grinned, his white teeth gleaming. He tapped Billy's shoulder. "You okay, Billy. If I could pitch like you, I could get rich." Then he got serious. "Hey, how you got that limp?"

"Gang fight," Billy said. I hoped Rico would be happy with that. I didn't need him getting upset about Keet Wilson. An eye for an eye was the way Rico went through life.

"Rich *haoles* don't get in no gang fights," Rico said, punching Billy's arm, but not hard. "Makes a good story, anyway, yeah?"

We scuffed into class and settled down in the back row, screeching our wooden desks on the floor as we fell into them.

• • •

Right after lunch, Rico, Mose, and Billy went outside and sat in the shade, but I went to talk to Mr. Ramos about my science project. I told him I wanted to do a demonstration on pigeons.

Mr. Ramos fingered his fat knuckle, which had never healed right after the fight downtown. "That's a good idea, Tomi, but what's so special about pigeons?" He smiled.

"You ever seen a tumbler fly?"

"Never even heard of a tumbler."

"So, there. That's a pigeon. Not many people have seen those kind. They do somersaults in the air . . . while they are flying. You wouldn't believe it. They go around and around and flip. It's crazy. Someone must have bred that into them hundreds of years ago. I'd like to research that and—"

"Okay, okay," Mr. Ramos said, putting his hands up. "How could I turn away that kind of enthusiasm? So . . . what about the rest of those juvenile delinquents you run around with? Are they even *thinking* about it?"

"Sure," I said. "But they don't want to talk about it. Someone might steal their ideas."

"I should have thought of that," Mr. Ramos said. "Well, get them to tell *me*. I won't steal them."

He was okay, Mr. Ramos.

And he was smart too. Mose told me that out of all his hundreds of relatives, Mr. Ramos was the only one who'd ever gotten a scholarship to college. And not only that, he got it from the famous University of Notre Dame. On the mainland.

Mose said Mr. Ramos was actually a lawyer, but he gave it up after his sixteen-year-old brother got arrested and sent to reform school for robbing a store. "It really got to him," Mose said. "He blamed himself, you know. He said he should have spent more time with his little brother. Maybe he could have prevented it."

So Mr. Ramos quit being a lawyer and went back to school to become a teacher. "Those boys out there need somebody *before,* not *after,* they get into trouble," Mr. Ramos told Rico's father. Rico's father said he was crazy, he'd make a lot more money as a lawyer. But Mr. Ramos said he would make enough as a teacher, and besides, money wasn't the reason he was doing it.

I didn't know anyone in school who wasn't glad he'd made that change.

"Shoot, you going be president of the U.S. someday," Rico said as I dropped down in the shade. "You just keep on kissing up to Mr. Uncle Ramos like that."

I shoved him with my elbow, and he shoved back, then we settled down into our usual talk about nothing important.

But something was bothering Billy. He leaned against the stucco building with his knees up and his elbows resting on them.

After a few minutes Mose nudged him. "You pretty quiet today, Billy. Something wrong?"

"Naw . . ."

"Come on, I can tell."

Billy glanced at Mose, then looked away. "I just hate to think I can't go to Roosevelt next year, that's all."

We were all quiet a moment. It was a junk thought. The four of us had been together a long time. It would sure be different when Billy was gone, even if we still saw each other after school.

"It's expensive, you know, that school," Rico said.

"Yeah," Mose added, "but *haoles* got the money."

"Some do," Billy said. "But *haoles* are just like anyone else—some poor, some rich, but most are just regular."

"No kidding," Rico said, shaking his head. I couldn't tell if he was joking or if it was really news to him.

Billy practically rubbed his hands raw, working the newness off the baseball, like he was mad at it, or something. After a while, he stopped rubbing and put the ball to his nose to smell it. "You guys ever heard of the *Greer*?"

Rico shrugged. "What's that?"

"A U.S. destroyer. Yesterday a German submarine shot at it. They didn't sink it, but they *shot* at it somewhere in the Atlantic."

Billy tossed the ball from hand to hand, frowning at it. "Do any of you . . ." He thought for a second, then went on. "Do any of you think we're going to get dragged into the war?"

Nobody said anything for a minute.

We all knew there was a war going on, but far away—between Japan and China. And also between Germany and France. Germany was winning and taking over all the countries around it. It was pretty bad, I knew that much. But I didn't really think about it. Not like Papa, anyway, who was very interested in it. And over at Billy's house I saw magazines that had war pictures in them—burned cars and trucks, and busted-up towns, and tired, beaten soldiers. They even showed pictures of dead people. I couldn't stop looking at those. But who wanted to think about it?

"Naah," Rico finally said. "Why us? The U.S. not bothering nobody."

"Keet Wilson told my brother that we'd be in the war before next summer," Billy said. "And he said we're all going to end up dead before we're twenty-one."

"Dead from what?" Mose asked.

"The Germans."

"Stupit," Rico said, shaking his head.

"Why?" Billy asked.

"Listen." Rico tapped Billy's arm with the back of his hand. "Even if we got in the war, look—just on this island we got the stupit army, we got the navy, we got the air force and even the marines. No Germans are going to last long against those guys. And we got soldiers all over the mainland, too, I bet."

Billy stared at his baseball, running the tip of his finger over the lacing. Rico was probably right. Army guys were all over the place. They had maneuvers all the time. Down on the west end of the island you could sometimes see smoke rising into the sky, with pursuit fighters above, circling like flies.

And last summer, Mr. Davis drove me and Billy up toward Wheeler Field and Schofield Barracks. You could see convoys of green trucks and jeeps raising dust on the red-dirt roads past the cane fields. We stopped to watch.

When Mr. Davis turned off the engine, you could hear shooting in the hills, little popping sounds and the rattle of machine-gun fire. It was strange to think of that going on while the rest of us went fishing and played baseball.

"Yeah," Billy said. "You're right . . . I guess it just feels funny that the Germans shot at one of *our* ships, that's all."

"Hey," Rico said to Billy. "I know what you can tell that guy . . . what's his name?"

"Keet."

"Anyway, tell him to go down to Pearl Harbor and look at one of those new aircraft carriers. *Big,* man, and they got plenty planes. All that guy has to do is see one of those things and his worries will be over."

"Yeah," Mose said, nodding. "And the army got howitzers and bazookas and more guns like that too."

"Shhh," Rico said. "Forget the stupit army. They just Boy Scouts."

"And what about the pursuit fighters?" I added. "They'd shoot any German ships before they could even get close to us."

Billy thought for a minute, holding the ball in the knuckle-ball grip. "I don't think Keet is worried about the war."

"Why not?" Rico asked.

Billy shrugged. "He likes that kind of stuff."

"What stuff?"

"Guns. Shooting things."

I wanted to add that if he liked it so much he should join the army. That would solve a lot of problems. But I kept my mouth shut. Papa might hear about it.

The Emperor

After school, Mose and Rico walked with me and Billy to the bus stop.

"Hey," Billy said, "thanks again for the ball."

"You earned it," Mose said. I think he was pleased that the ball had meant so much to Billy.

Rico flicked his eyebrows like that Groucho guy in the movies, then he and Mose continued on down the road to where they lived.

Tough Boy Gary Ferris, who was third baseman on the Rats, caught up and joined them. Tough Boy was built like a garbage can. He was short and had big muscles, and was held in high esteem by Rico, because he was the younger brother of Tina, who lived in Rico's dreams as his future girlfriend. The three of them walked away like they were on a rocking boat, bumping into each other with their shoulders.

I followed Billy onto the bus, the last two in line. We squeezed our way to the back. Everyone knew our seat, so nobody was sitting there. Billy stared out the window and tossed his new baseball from one hand to the other.

I started reading my science homework, but my mind kept wandering back to my same old daydream of how it would feel to beat up Keet Wilson. Sometimes I wanted that so bad, just to punch him once, or even just to shove him, if that's all I could get away with before he smashed me into the dirt. Sometimes it was almost impossible to just swallow trouble the way Papa demanded. *If you make trouble and lose face,* he told me so many times that I heard it in my sleep, *you shame yourself. If you shame yourself, you shame all of us. Be above it, Tomi . . . that's the only way.*

Criminy. He must have been made out of steel.

We got off near the grocery store at the bottom of the valley and hiked up to where we lived, on a narrow road with big white houses hidden back in the trees. When we passed Keet's house, Billy and I both glanced up the long, curved driveway. You could see the porch and the glass windows on the first floor, but the top half was hidden in the jungle of trees between the road and the house. Somewhere in there, Mama was mopping the floors or making somebody's bed.

Before we got to Billy's house we headed into the trees, following the dirt path that stumbled through the weeds and jungle to my house in the far corner of the Wilson estate. Keet called it a shack. But Papa said if our house was a shack, then where he grew up back in Japan was a chicken coop.

When Lucky saw us coming, she dragged herself up

and trotted down to meet us, walking stiff-legged and crooked, her belly poking out to the sides. Her tail stood straight up, like a flagpole. She was supposed to be called Rocky, but no one in my family could say that word. *Locky* was the best they could do. So I changed it to Lucky. Anyway, Billy told me she was mostly beagle. But she could have been mostly lizard and it wouldn't have made any difference to me. Papa found her down by his boat and she was the best present he'd ever given me.

"Boy, she getting kind of fat," I said.

I stopped and bent down to pet her, then looked around the yard. Quiet. Kimi and Grampa were probably up by his chickens.

Lucky leaned against Billy's leg, then scratched her belly, her hind leg flying. Billy reached down and rubbed her neck. Lucky yawned, her eyes stretching to slits.

Billy waited out in the yard with Lucky while I went up the stairs and into the house. In all the years I'd known him, he'd never asked if he could come inside. I guess I could understand that—Mama didn't encourage it. And I guess I didn't either. Mama was a very private person.

But for me it was different. I was kind of embarrassed, mostly about my room. Billy's room was three times bigger, at least. And when I was at his house, his mother never made me feel anything but welcome. She was a nurse at Queen's Hospital and wasn't always home, but when she was, she always asked about Mama and Papa. And even Grampa, sometimes. Then she'd help us find a snack and send us up to Billy's room where we'd sit around and look at magazines.

At my house we didn't even have *one* magazine. All I

had in my room was Grampa's tatami mat on the floor and four orange crates me and Grampa shared. We stacked them up and put our clothes in them. And I had a metal bed that was only a mattress on a wire mesh attached to the frame by rusty metal coils that squeaked. It was the only bed in the house. Everyone else slept on the floor, like in Japan.

Under my bed, wrapped in a silky *furoshiki* scarf and a burlap bag, was Grampa's treasure—the family *katana,* or samurai sword. He even had an oil cloth neatly folded in a box in the burlap bag, to keep the blade sharp and clean. The *katana* had been in our family for over three hundred years. Grampa wasn't sure, but he thought someone had been killed by it a long time ago.

If I ever became worthy, Grampa said, he would pass it down to me. He spent many hours telling me about how important it was, trying to prepare me for the day he would hand it to me to be its keeper and protector. It was our most prized possession, he said, the symbol of generations of honorable living in our family. Thinking about all that responsibility made me nervous, and Grampa could probably see that. I wanted to show it to Billy so much, I almost had to tie my hands behind my back. But it was sacred, and I couldn't treat it like just some toy.

Grampa told me that in the olden days if you dropped it or mishandled it you would have gotten your head chopped off. Those things were made to the highest perfection. They had their own spirits, almost. And even though my devotion to the family wasn't good enough for Grampa, I knew how important that *katana* was. It wasn't just a sharp blade that he hid under my bed. It was the heart of our history. Grampa honored it and protected it. So did Papa. And so would I.

I threw my science book on the bed and changed into an old shirt.

Billy suddenly rapped on the front door, which was only a rusty screen. It rattled like it was about to fall off. "Tomi," he called. "Come out here."

I hurried out.

"What?" I said.

"I got a surprise for you. I don't think Lucky got fat. . . . She's going to have puppies."

"What?"

"Really, come feel her sides."

Lucky stared up at us, looking guilty and innocent at the same time, blinking her eyes and wagging her whole rear end. Her sides felt as solid as a hundred-pound tuna. "Shee, must be from Rufus. That's the only boy dog around here." Rufus was Keet's German shepherd.

"Maybe, but Rufus is pretty big to be fooling around with a beagle."

"Who else, then?"

Billy shrugged. "I want one of the pups, okay?"

"You better take them all or else Grampa might drown them."

"He wouldn't do that . . . would he?"

"Who can tell with him? One time, he wanted to put Lucky in a rice bag and take her out to sea because she chased his chickens. Anyway, you can have the first pick."

Imagine that, Lucky was going to have pups. I would have to act upset about it around Papa and Grampa, but inside I would be purring like a cat.

I gave Lucky a hug and she licked my face.

"Get your mitt," Billy said. "Let's go."

I went back inside to get the glove. When I came out of my room, Billy was waiting at the open screen door, looking around our small front room. It was spotlessly neat. Mama didn't like any messes.

"What's all that? Who's in that picture?" he said, nodding over to our family *butsudan,* a black boxlike thing with doors that opened to a small stage. If you stood up the giant dictionary in the school library, it would be about that big, only much lighter. Anyway, on the stage inside the *butsudan* was a small photograph of my grandmother.

"That's . . . kind of like an altar . . . to remember Grandma by. That's her in that picture."

"Why's she in an altar?"

What could I say?

"Well . . . she died, and Grampa . . . Grampa talks to her."

"Talks to her?"

"He does it all the time. And he lights some incense for her when the sun rises and when it sets. Every day. See, her spirit gives him guidance, and protection. That's what Mama says. The *butsudan* is a place you can go to, when you need some help, when you have a problem."

"The same as going to church?"

"I guess so. Anyway, it's very important. Especially for Grampa."

"You believe in that?"

"Yeah, sort of. . . . I guess. . . . I don't know."

Billy studied it a moment, then looked up at the picture of Emperor Hirohito on the wall above it. The emperor was like the king of Japan, standing in the photograph as stiff as a glass doll. He wore wooden shoes with high bottoms, and a heavy-looking robe. And a hat with a foot-long feather thing standing straight up on top. Funny-looking. But back in the olden days, where that stuff came from, it was very elegant. At least, Grampa said it was.

"That's the emperor of Japan," I said.

"What's that thing on his head?"

"Who knows? Crazy, yeah?"

"Looks like a rooster."

I grabbed a couple of apples from the fruit bowl by the couch and tossed one to Billy. "Go get your glove. . . . I'll meet you at diamond grass in ten minutes. I better go look for Grampa and tell him where to find me. And bring that new ball."

Billy jumped off the porch and jogged through the trees toward his house. Lucky came up the steps and peeked in the door, her ears cocked. "How we going tell Papa about all those pups, you crazy dog?"

I shook my head and turned back to the emperor. I'd seen him so often, I'd almost forgotten he was there.

• • •

We met at the field where the pigeon lofts were. Diamond grass, Billy called it, a field between his house and mine, a green, grassy place where we went to practice baseball and get away from the world. Being there was like being on a small boat where the world shrinks down to a few feet of wood and everything works just the way you want it to. I guess you could say it was our refuge. Billy came up with that name because the whole place looked like diamonds in the morning when the grass was sparkling with dewdrops and the sun was shining on it.

Billy jogged out from between the trees and threw me the ball, a high pop-fly. I caught it with my bare hand.

"Hoo, a baseball legend," Billy said.

"You right about that, *haole* boy."

We tossed the ball back and forth a few minutes to warm up. I tried to copy the way he threw, relaxed and smooth. But Billy had a special way I just couldn't seem to match. When he pitched, the ball always hit my glove solid. He was a natural.

Billy was back to his old easy self again, not quiet like on the bus. I figured he must have been worried about the attack on the *Greer*. I kind of was too. I could almost see Hitler gobbling up countries like Mr. Ramos said he was doing.

"Okay," Billy said, walking over to the mound. It was really just a small pile of dirt that Billy and I wheelbarrowed over from Billy's garden. And for home plate, we cut out a piece of plywood, then got a sickle to make the grass short between the mound and the plate. It was a pretty good setup.

Billy put the ball in his glove and raked his hair back with his fingers. "Curveball today . . . that's all I'm going to throw. . . . So, what's the sign?"

"Two fingers."

"Okay, let's go."

Billy leaned forward and stared at me, the ball behind his back.

I punched my mitt and squatted behind the plate. "Boy, those Kaka'ako guys sure got mad when they saw you could throw those curves."

"Yep," Billy said.

Billy's father said it wasn't a good idea to start throwing curveballs until you were thirteen or fourteen, because you could hurt your arm permanently. So Billy waited, because he wanted to do things right. This year the *haole* school baseball coach, who'd had his eye on Billy, had finally said he could start trying out the curve. So now Billy had four pitches—fastball, fastball change, curveball, and curveball change. That's how we beat the Kaka'ako Boys for the first time in the last six games.

Billy let one fly. *Whomp.* Square in my glove. Solid. Stung my hand. I tossed back the ball.

"Okay, let's get to work," Billy said.

He was a workhorse. When *he* practiced, *I* practiced. He wouldn't even let my *mind* take a break. I crouched down behind the plate and gave the sign—two fingers.

Billy nodded. I could imagine the Dodgers—Whit Wyatt nodding to Mickey Owen. I moved up into the catching position, eyes level, wrist loose. Billy wound up and let one fly.

Whomp!

I threw it back. "Low. Try again."

Whomp!

"Not bad . . . for a *haole*."

Whomp! Whomp! Whomp! For the next half hour he

pitched curveballs. We hardly said a word. My legs ached, but it felt good. We were getting better, tighter.

The Kaka'ako Boys usually beat us because they were more serious about baseball than the lazy bums we had. They were all from the Japanese part of Kaka'ako, an area crammed with old buildings down in the hot and dusty part of town.

The place was poor and pretty rickety. Japanese, Hawaiians, and Portuguese lived there, but separated into their own sections. I loved it down there. Lots of action. Lots of people in the streets, and stores, and things like that. Not like where me and Billy lived on the quiet streets of Nu'uanu Valley where rich people lived, mostly *haoles*. Kaka'ako was a different world. Or maybe *we* lived in the different world. More of Honolulu was like Kaka'ako than Nu'uanu. Down there you found the people who did the hard kind of work—cannery workers, fishermen, truck drivers, boat builders, tuna packer guys, and the men who worked on the roads.

Whomp!

Whomp!

Almost an hour of curveballs.

"Let's take a break," I finally said. My legs felt like two rusty door hinges.

"Not yet . . . Ten minutes, that's all . . . ten minutes."

We went for almost a half hour more before Billy decided to rest his arm.

A slight breeze combed through the treetops as the island cooled down. The sun, now lower in the sky, sent long, jagged shadows across the field. Billy tucked the ball into his glove and flopped down to the grass. "So who's going to take the Series?"

"Brooklyn," I said.

Billy shook his head. "You're dreaming, *compadre*. The Yanks will chew 'em up and spit 'em out."

"Nope."

"Hey. They're hot, *way* hot."

"But the Dodgers got Reiser . . . batting .343."

"You want to back that up with something more than words?"

"Ten cents," I said. "Kiss it good-bye."

Billy stuck out his hand. "Make it fifteen and you're on, sucker." We sealed it with a shake.

A shadow startled me. I squinted up into Grampa's face. He leaned over me and Billy with his shiny bald head, shaved clean in the old traditional Japanese way.

Billy bolted up when he saw him.

Grampa grinned. But his smile turned into his usual scowl when he looked back at me. "Papa home. Get up. He like you come clean fish."

"He's not supposed to be back until tomorrow."

"Home now, confonnit." Grampa turned and started walking back to the house.

Billy stood, keeping his eyes on Grampa, still wary.

"I gotta go," I said.

Just then Papa came strolling through the trees. "The fish can wait," he told Grampa, who just went right on past Papa as if he hadn't even seen him there.

Papa had short black hair, army style. His face was sun-brown and his eyes crinkled at the edges. He walked up to us wearing a white undershirt, and wrinkled khaki pants like Grampa's. He flicked his eyebrows to Billy, then smiled and put his rough hand on my shoulder. "How you boys doing? How's those girlfrens?"

Billy looked down. He was too shy for girls, and I guess I was too. But there was a girl I thought was pretty cute—Donna, in Mr. Ramos's class. But I never told *her* that. Anyway, Billy and I were too busy playing baseball for girls.

Papa grinned and scruffed Billy's hair. "Ne'mind, then. How's the birds?"

"Okay," I said.

Papa smelled like fish and sweat. His khaki pants were crusty where he'd wiped a couple of days of fish slime off his hands.

"You fly 'um yet?"

"No."

"Let's go, then." With his hand still on my shoulder, we went over to one of the lofts, the split one—one side tumblers and racers, and the other side high-fliers and some captives for breeding. The high-fliers were Papa's favorites, though he spent more time with the racers. He liked the tumblers, too, because they amazed him when they did their flips while flying around in circles.

Papa studied the birds awhile, then said, "Go lie in grass. . . . I going let out high ones."

Me and Billy moved out to the center of the field. Papa opened the loft door and tapped the side lightly. Six high-fliers exploded out, almost too fast to see, wings flapping, beating against each other, bursting into brilliant whites and grays when they flew above the trees into the sunlight. A faint feathery dust followed them out.

Papa came over and lay in the grass next to us. No one spoke, we just watched the birds climb into the sky. Those birds flew so high I thought they would pop. Soon they became specks. Straight up, higher than even the bravest clouds would go, it seemed.

I tried to imagine being one of them, floating in the sky with the wind pushing up under the fan of my wings, rumbling in my ears. I'd look down and see me and Billy and Papa like ants in the field far below, and the shiny silver roof of our house, and Keet's and Billy's houses nearby. And then the cemetery past the trees, that whole city of gravestones in one view. You could see so much it would make you dizzy.

"Mama should see these birds," Papa said, mostly to himself.

I peeked over at him. Mama once told me there was no one else in the whole world like Papa. "We all very lucky, Tomi-kun," she said.

One day when Grampa was in a dreamy mood because his friend, Charlie, had given him a green bottle of *sake*, Japanese rice wine, he told me the story of how Mama and Papa met.

When she was only sixteen, Mama sailed over from Japan to marry a sugarcane worker. She was one of those picture brides—she'd never even met the guy except through a picture and a couple of letters. In those days that was the only way a Japanese man in Hawaii could meet a Japanese woman, and lots of people did it. I told Mama it seemed like a big gamble, but she said it was a way to get out of the poverty she'd grown up in, which was worse than any I would ever see in Honolulu.

So Mama sailed over with hundreds of other picture brides to meet her new husband and start a new life.

But before she got here, the guy was killed in a gambling fight. Mama got off the boat and no one was there to take her in. She ended up staying with a fisherman who had sent for a bride from the same ship. Mama's story spread quickly around the fishing boats, Grampa said. The poor girl. What she going do? Sell herself in a bar for the navy guys? When Papa heard the story, he found the fisherman and asked if could meet the bride with no husband. Papa was kind of lonely, Grampa said.

"Just think about that, Tomi-kun," Mama said. "If he never did that, how sad would my life be. . . . I would probably have sailed back home . . . alone. Unwanted bride. Then who would marry me?"

I looked back up at the high-fliers, now almost invisible. So high. So sure of themselves, like Papa. I wondered if I could ever be like him.

5

The P-40 Tomahawks

"Tomi," Papa said early one Saturday morning a couple of weeks later. He nudged me and I sat up. A kerosene lamp, turned low, hung from his fingers.

"Okay . . . I'm awake."

Papa nodded and set the lamp on the floor near Grampa's mat, which was empty. Then he left.

For a moment I stared at the wall, not awake, but not asleep. The lantern made the whole room glow an orangy-brown that made getting up that early worth it, just to get the feeling. Papa and Grampa probably felt like that, too, because they *never* got up after the sun.

I rubbed my eyes and squinted at the clock by my bed. Three forty-five.

A pair of shorts and an old shirt. That's all I'd need,

because we'd only be gone two days. I got dressed and took the lantern out to the kitchen, where Mama was heating up the kerosene stove. The sweet smell of the flame filled the room. Mama smiled at me.

The screen door to the backyard squeaked in the blackness as I went out. The trees and jungle loomed gray and spooky in the light from the lantern. Lucky sat at the bottom of the stairs looking up, whining and wagging her tail.

"Go back to sleep," I said, walking down the stairs. "You're just wasting your time." Papa would sooner carry bad-luck bananas on his boat than Lucky, who would leave little puddles around the deck. Besides, Papa was already taking a chance on bad luck by letting me bring Billy along this time. It would be the first time a *haole* had ever even set foot on the *Taiyo Maru*. Maybe it would even be the first time a *haole* set foot on *any* Japanese fishing boat. Papa's helper, Sanji, said *haoles* were bad luck.

"Where the boy?" Papa asked as he came out of the darkness of the path that led to the outhouse.

"He'll be here," I said.

Papa nodded and went up the back steps to the kitchen.

I held the lantern high to spread the light around. The shadows in the trees moved as I crept into the jungle. The air smelled sweet, full of some kind of flower you could only smell at night. I took a deep breath and tried to remember it.

But when I got near the outhouse my memory went blank. That place was just a deep hole in the ground surrounded by a wooden closet with bugs inside, the kind that live in the dark and run for it in the light.

I held my breath and went in. I almost made it without breathing. Hoo, that place smelled like a grave, or something. The air smelled twice as sweet when I ran back out.

It was going to be a great day. . . . I could feel it.

"Ssssst," someone whispered from the blackness, and I jumped.

Billy came smiling into the small circle of light.

"Jeese! Don't scare me like that, confonnit."

"Look," he said, handing me a pair of binoculars. "Dad said we could use them."

They were black and heavy. I looked through them but couldn't see anything, then handed them back.

Billy stuffed the binoculars into a small canvas bag that hung from his shoulder. He smelled like toothpaste.

"You had breakfast yet?" I asked.

"Nope."

I picked up the lantern and started toward the house. "Come on, then."

You could see Mama and Papa working in the kitchen through the screen window. Billy stopped and waited at the bottom of the steps while I went up. "Come inside," I said, turning back. It was only the kitchen.

Papa came to the door carrying a metal bucket with a lid on it. He lifted the bucket to show Billy. "Bait . . . fresh opelu . . . Charlie went catch 'um." Papa squeezed past me and started down the stairs.

Billy stepped back so Papa could get by. "Mr. Nakaji . . ." Billy said. "Thank you for inviting—"

"Nah," Papa said, butting in. " 'S okay." Papa was a lot more friendly to Billy than Mama was. He was friendly to everyone. It drove Grampa crazy, because he wanted Papa to be more firm, like he was. And anyway, Grampa wasn't too sure Papa should let me mix with *haoles*.

Billy nodded.

Papa smiled and said, "Go inside, you boys. Eat. I going get birds." Papa always took a couple of racers out on the boat to let them fly home, to keep them in shape.

Billy came inside and sat on the edge of a chair at the kitchen table. He was barefoot, like I was, so he didn't have to take his shoes off. I glanced at Mama's face to see how she felt about Papa's invitation to Billy to come inside and eat. But Mama looked just like always, kind of serious, but not worried about anything, as far as I could tell.

Mama brought us each a steaming bowl of rice, and in another, smaller bowl, a raw egg. Then she poured some shoyu into the bowl with the egg and whipped it around with her cooking chopsticks. Raw egg and soy sauce. My mouth was watering. Billy watched with big wide fish eyes. "It's good," I said, to reassure him. "Eggs don't get much fresher than this."

Mama poured the shoyu-egg over our sticky rice and gave us some chopsticks.

Billy waited, staring at the bowl in front of him. He picked up the chopsticks and tried to make them work.

"Itadakimasu," I said, and Billy looked up.

"It's what you say before you eat," I said.

"What's it mean?"

"It means, let's eat."

I mashed the rice and shoyu-egg together and dug in. Billy poked around the eggs, trying to keep the rice and egg separate. He managed to balance a few bits of eggless rice on the ends of his chopsticks. I tried to keep from laughing. It was good to finally have him come into our house for more than just a couple of minutes. Maybe I'd think about letting him see my room someday. . . . *Maybe.*

Pretty soon Grampa came in the back door with more fresh eggs from his chickens. He seemed to be in a good mood. He tipped his head toward the bucket of eggs and glanced at Billy. "Good, nah?"

Billy nodded. He looked nervous, and I had to smile. Grampa always made Billy kind of shaky, and Grampa knew it. "You seasick today?" Grampa asked Billy.

"Grampa!"

"I hope not," Billy answered. "Never have been before, anyway."

Grampa put the eggs by the sink and sat down next to Billy.

Billy stopped picking at his rice.

Mama poured Grampa a cup of tea. I just hoped he wouldn't start slurping it in front of Billy. Criminy, sometimes he sounded like Lucky drinking water.

Papa's voice sliced through the nighttime stillness from outside. "Sanji coming soon. . . . You boys ready?"

"Ready," I said, pushing my chair back and gulping the last bite of gooey, sweet rice. *"Gochisoh-sama."*

Billy stood up, half the rice still on his plate. "It means you're done eating," I said.

Grampa glanced at Billy's uneaten rice, then at Billy. With his arms resting on the table, Grampa clenched and flexed his jaw, and made his lips curl back to suck air in through his teeth. The tendons in his neck stood out like wires. Mama always told us never to leave even one grain of rice on the table, that it was a small treasure, that a farmer went through a lot of trouble to grow it.

Billy glanced at me.

"He's just telling you that if you want to be a muscle man like he is you gotta eat all your rice. Come on, let's go."

Billy pushed past me and hurried out.

"Che," Grampa mumbled under his breath.

Yup, it was going to be a great day, all right.

• • •

Sanji met us out on the road, his old fishy-smelling truck rattling as it idled, or tried to idle, anyway. He had to pump on the gas pedal every time it sounded like it was about to die. Sanji nodded to me and Billy, a big grin on his face, as if taking Billy along was the craziest thing he'd ever done. It probably was.

Billy climbed into the back, and I handed him the wooden crate that held Papa's two racers. I jumped in after him. Papa handed me the bucket of bait and a box of sweet specialties that Mama had made for us to eat on the boat. "Let's go," Papa said to Sanji as he slid into the cab.

Sanji worked hard for that truck. Papa said he had two other part-time jobs besides fishing. The only problem with Sanji's truck was the fishy stink, which stuck to you like sunburn. But Sanji was very lucky. Not many fishermen had a truck.

The streets were deserted and silent. Only a few lights were on in the dark houses we passed. The slightest hint of morning edged up over the mountains behind us, a faint purple-black glow. Sanji only had to restart the truck twice before we got down to Kewalo Basin, where Papa kept the *Taiyo Maru.*

As usual, Sanji had already gotten the boat ready. When did that guy sleep? There was ice in the fish box and four buckets of fishing line set out on the deck. He'd also filled the wooden keg with fresh drinking water. We'd only be gone two days this time, because we couldn't miss school, so the one bucket of bait Papa brought along would be enough.

Papa and Sanji looked like twins in their long khaki pants and white BVD tank tops. Sanji even had a ballahead haircut, like Papa.

Papa put the bait in the iced fish box, then fired up the old diesel engine, which made a lot of racket in the quiet harbor. We were lucky to have diesel. Some boats still ran on kiawe wood, where you had to keep a hot fire going all the time.

Sanji took the crate with the pigeons aboard and put it by the deckhouse, where the birds would be out of the wind. "What they call you?" Sanji asked, passing by Billy.

"Billy."

"Okay. So, Billy. You ever been on one boat?"

"Only ocean liners . . . my dad works for Matson."

"Hoo," Sanji said, making big eyes like he was impressed. Matson was the biggest shipping line in Hono-lulu, maybe even the whole Pacific Ocean.

"Well, anyway," Sanji went on, "the main thing is no fall off, yeah? Easy to fall in the water from this boat."

Papa's sampan was about thirty feet long, mostly a flat, open deck with a small deckhouse toward the front where the engine was. Papa steered from a long-armed wooden tiller in the back. There was no shelter. You couldn't even get out of the sun unless you went down into the fish box under the deckhouse, or else Papa hung the tarp up for shade. But the box made you sick just to smell it, and Papa never put up the tarp unless it was raining. He never thought to get out of the sun. He and Sanji didn't even wear hats, which is why Papa's face was ten times browner than the skin under his shirt and had a lot of lines on it, especially by his eyes.

"I can keep myself aboard," Billy said.

Sanji nodded, and tapped Billy's shoulder. "Good . . . One boy in the ocean hard to find."

Sanji was only nineteen, but he seemed much older. I guess it was because he was married already, and he had that truck and was working. "His parents must have been a couple of jokers," I whispered. "Sanji means 'three o'clock.' "

Billy peeked over at Sanji.

"And he's got a three-year-old daughter, you know, which means he was only three years older than *us* when she was born."

Billy shook his head, and whispered, "Wow . . ."

Papa thought Sanji was the greatest thing since diesel engines. He knew the ocean as well as anyone, Papa said.

And Sanji was a good swimmer and he had courage, which sometimes came in handy. Like one time when they got a line wrapped up in the prop and Sanji went down to cut it loose or else they would have been stuck out there until somebody found them. When Sanji got in the water some sharks came nosing around and Papa had to throw chunks of fish meat out to them to keep them away. And Sanji just kept on working under the hull.

I'd gone out on the boat lots of times, but I still worried because Papa didn't have a radio, so he couldn't call for help if we needed it. He couldn't afford one. He said he was lucky just to make the payments on the boat. But with no radio . . . What if the engine broke? What if the prop got jammed? What if a shark had gotten Sanji that day?

We finished loading up, and Papa walked the boat out of the black harbor. Even at that early hour, we passed fishermen squatting like toads on the rocks with their bamboo poles. Sanji waved at one of them, his deaf cousin. The shadowy man lifted his chin.

Papa aimed the *Taiyo Maru* for open sea. The ocean was as smooth as melting ice, and the lights on shore shimmered out over the dark water like wobbly palm trees.

Papa stood at the tiller, guiding it with his knee while he rummaged through a bucket of line, checking the hooks and sinkers. The boat rose and fell in the dark, smooth and easy, slicing the morning water. The engine chugged and vibrated in the floorboards and spat out smoky bubbles in the wake.

"This is a good place, Tomikazu," Papa suddenly said. "Smell that sweet air."

I faced into the breeze and took a long, thirsty breath. Sweet like the jungle. Clean, and rich with salt.

"*Ii-na.* Good, nah?" Papa said.

I nodded. "Good."

• • •

In an hour's time the sun had colored the ocean silver, then deep, deep blue. And you could see puffy white clouds sitting stone-still way out on the horizon, where we were headed. Now, far behind, the purple-green island drew down into the sea as if it were sinking, looking like one pretty good wave could just roll right on over it.

"Tomi," Papa said, slowing the boat down to a crawl. He pointed his chin toward the racers. "Let 'um go."

Billy and I set the box in the center of the deck and each lifted a pigeon out, holding them the way Papa had taught me, and I had taught Billy—with the feet tucked between the second and third finger and the belly cupped in the palm of the hand. Mine was gray, with a white neck. Billy's was all rusty red.

The pigeon seemed to hum in my hand, eager to fly. I put its solid body next to my cheek, and smelled the musty feathers. "See you tomorrow night, bird," I whispered.

Me and Billy glanced at each other, then threw the pigeons into the air with easy sweeping motions. The birds fluttered out, then rose into the sky. They circled the boat once and raced back toward the island.

Billy got his binoculars out and watched them, with Sanji breathing down his neck. "What's that?" Sanji asked.

"Binoculars."

"Oh, yeah. I heard of it."

"*Heard* of them? You mean you've never looked through binoculars before?"

Sanji laughed. "Who I know got that thing?"

Billy handed the binoculars to Sanji, who thought they were a miracle. He put his hand out and looked at his fingers. "Ho!"

"Look at the island," Billy said, turning Sanji so he faced the right way. "Ho!" Sanji said again.

When Papa wanted to look through them, he had to wrestle them away from Sanji. Papa smiled under the binoculars as he studied the island, then the birds getting smaller and smaller, and the ocean all around the boat, and the clouds on the horizon. He even looked at *me*. I had to keep sticking my hand in front of the lenses to get them back.

"Hey," Billy said, tapping my shoulder. "Look."

A silver dot on the horizon, growing larger, fast. A single pursuit fighter, flying low and heading straight toward the boat.

Billy took the binoculars from Papa and raised them to his eyes. "P-40. Tomahawk."

Another plane appeared from the left and banked in to join the first one. Silently, they flew toward us, their shadows racing over the surface of the sea. Then the rumble of their engines, coming louder and louder.

Papa started waving at them.

"He always make like that," Sanji said, hooking a thumb at Papa. "Just like one kid."

"Let me *see*," I said, tugging on Billy's arm. The planes were almost to the boat.

Just as the fighters reached us, the pilots wagged their wings, then pulled up. They climbed into the sky, circled stars under silver wings flashing down like lightning. The engines roared so loud, the air around the boat seemed to shake. The noise shivered through the decking, up through my feet and into my legs.

"Hoo," Papa said, shading his eyes with his hand as they headed past toward the island. "I wish this old tub had those engines."

The fighters faded toward the island landscape, gray specks losing themselves against the barely visible sugar-cane and pineapple fields.

"Probably heading for Wheeler Field," Billy said, putting the binoculars back in the bag.

"You see lots of those planes out here," Sanji said. "Before, got one, two a week. But now, get maybe ten times that in one day. Bombye this whole island's going be only army mens."

"It's because of the war," Billy said.

"What war?"

"The one in Europe, and China. That's why we got so many ships and planes and soldiers here."

"But no more war here," Sanji said.

Billy frowned and looked back toward the island.

6

The Crowded Sea

We headed right into a swarm of seabirds circling and rising high into the sky, then falling to the sea, making small white explosions when they hit.

"Those birds called *noio*," Sanji said. "They feeding on those small fish you see flying from the water. But under them, is *aku*."

A school of flying fish the size of three baseball fields skipped over the sea in a frenzy, trying to escape the birds above and the feeding *aku* below. There were nine other boats already there, all Japanese sampans. Papa and the men on the other boats raised their chins to each other.

"*Aku?*" Billy asked.

"The *haoles* call 'um skipjack tuna," Sanji said.

Papa made a wide loop around the school and waited in their path. We would drift quietly toward them as they fed against the current. The other boats drifted, too, so they wouldn't scare the fish down.

When the action hit, flying fish started landing on deck. We could use them for bait if the *aku* didn't go for the opelu we'd brought along. It was wild. I loved it when it got like that.

"Tomi," Papa said. "You and Billy use the buckets. We going use poles."

Sanji had cut the bait into raw strips while the sampan had chugged out to the birds. All you had to do was grab a chunk of opelu and stick it on the hook. When the fish were feeding like that you didn't even have to worry about hiding the steel.

Papa and Sanji grabbed the bamboo poles and tried fishing with no bait. Sometimes the *aku* went for the flashing silver.

Bam!

The *aku* hit.

"Hooie!" Papa yelled. "They grab anything!"

I ran for the two five-gallon buckets of line and gave one to Billy.

"Put the bait on like this," I said, stabbing a hook as big as my finger through a strip of opelu. I threw it over the side and let the sinker pull it down. "Maybe there are some yellowfins down there."

Something hit my bait within seconds, then sank like a boulder. The line whipped out of the bucket and I had to let it run freely. With a hand line there was just you and the line. No fishing pole to help you.

Whatever had taken my bait was *big*. The line snapped out of the bucket. I couldn't stop it. My hands were too soft, not thick and leathery like Papa's. I grabbed a pair of canvas gloves.

Billy dropped his bait over. *Bam!* Both our lines were popping over the side, going down, down . . . way down.

"*What do I do? What do I do?*" Billy yelled, jumping around on the deck.

"Get some gloves! Over there, by the mallet."

Billy got the gloves and yanked them on, then started slapping his hand down on the line. It wasn't the way to stop it, but who cared. At a time like that you did what you could.

I finally managed to get a grip on my line. The power on the other end was stronger than any twenty-pound *aku.* This one had to be more like a hundred, at least.

The fish jerked away and the line ran through my gloves. It felt like it would saw right through and cut my fingers off.

"*Jeeze!*" Billy said, the line leaping out of his bucket like it was alive.

Again I managed to stop the run, wrapping the line once around my glove and hanging on, letting the fish know it was hooked, letting it calm down. Off to my right, I could see Papa and Sanji sailing *akus* over their heads like they were shoveling dirt. Papa's wet arms bulged and glistened in the sun. There had to be at least thirty blue and silver skipjacks in the fish box and flopping around on the deck.

"I can't stop the line!" Billy yelled.

"Just grab it," I said. "Don't worry, it won't go through your gloves."

He had to stop it soon or it would take all day to haul that fish back up to the boat. The line made sawing sounds as it zipped away under Billy's gloves. Finally he grabbed it, wincing. He was probably thinking about losing his fingers. That would end his pitching days.

"Tomi," Papa yelled. "Get the stick for Billy. . . . Put 'um in the side."

I kicked the Y-shaped stick over to Billy, a tough fork of kiawe wood worn smooth by years of fishing. "Put that in the hole in the side of the boat and wrap the line around it once."

Billy managed to get the line around the fork and stop the fish.

"Criminy," he said. "What's on the other end of this?"

"Something bigger than those things Papa and Sanji are catching," I said. "Mine too."

While Billy rested, I worked at pulling my fish up, inch by inch, dropping the line back into the bucket. Even through the gloves I could feel its smallest movements racing like electricity up the line and into my fingers. I stared down into the blue-black ocean for a glimpse of silver.

Nothing.

Papa and Sanji were soaked in sweat and seawater, and still pulling up *akus* like they were picking stones out of a garden. They didn't say a word to each other. *Akus* thunked on the deck behind me. Some slid over and flapped around my feet.

Billy tried pulling in on his line, but had to rest every

few minutes. "Whatever this is," he said, "it weighs more than a truck."

It took me about ten minutes to get my fish near the boat. When I first saw it shimmering below, I thought it was small. But it grew larger as I pulled it closer. I could see flashing silver, and dark blue, and a bright yellow line.

"I got an *ahi,*" I yelled over to Papa, who suddenly appeared at my side.

"They gone," he said, meaning the school. I looked up and could see the birds swarming off about a quarter mile. The other boats were scattered now, some following the school. I hadn't even seen them leave.

Sanji threw the *akus* into the fish box. Papa got the ones by my feet and tossed them across the deck toward him, then brought the hardwood mallet, the gaff, and a knife over by me. "When you get 'um close, I grab the line."

My fingers were cramping and about to fall off. Every time the yellowfin got close to the boat it jerked away, the line slipping through my fingers. It kept kicking, and bolting, taking about twenty feet of line every time. But I could feel it losing power.

I finally got it to where it was just below the gunwale. Papa leaned over and wrapped the line around his bare hand. With the gaff in the other hand, he hooked the curved steel under the gill. The yellowfin went crazy, flapping in the water, soaking the deck. Papa's face turned red as he pulled up on the gaff, trying to get the fish's head far enough out of the water to club it. He let go of the line and grabbed the mallet and whacked down.

Bok! Bok! Bok! Bok! Bok! Papa straining, water splashing and flying all over the place.

My claw-shaped fingers felt like they'd never open again.

Finally the yellowfin shivered and stopped slapping at the water. Power drained from its dying body. Papa threw down the mallet and grabbed the razor-sharp fish knife by his feet. In one quick motion, he cut a long slice under the tuna's gills. Brilliant red blood streamed into the blue water. A dark cloud spread around the side of the boat. You had to bleed a big fish like that after a fight, so the hot blood wouldn't burn the meat.

Finally Papa dragged it on board. It flopped to the deck, still shuddering. The beauty of those fish always amazed me. Glistening silver sides with a blue-black top and brilliant yellow fins. Fat and firm, like a hundred-pound bag of rice. It was a shame to take them from the sea, but I never said that in front of Papa or Sanji.

"Hoo," Papa said, then whistled. "I think maybe eighty, eighty-five pounds."

Sanji threw seawater on the deck to wash away the fish slime. "Not bad, Tomi," he said. "Someday maybe you going be good like your daddy, yeah?"

I dragged the yellowfin over and shoved it into the fish box.

"So what you waiting for? Pull 'um up," Sanji said to Billy, who looked as sorry as a sick dog. I guess I would have felt like that, too, if my fish was that far down. The line in his bucket was almost gone. Billy looped it around his glove and tried tugging it up. It moved, but not much. I shook my head, but kept my mouth shut. He probably had a couple hundred yards to pull back to the boat. Billy inched it in a little more, then rested.

"Let me feel 'um," Papa said. He pulled on Billy's line, shaking his head. "This one . . . chee . . . this one went straight down." Papa looked over at Sanji and winked. "You think this boy can pull 'um?"

"I don't know. . . . He tall, but skinny. What you think, Tomi?"

"Well . . ."

Billy glowered over at me.

"Shoot, yeah," I said. "Of course he can pull it up."

"Okay," Papa said, letting go of the line. "Bring 'um in . . . but no take all day, yeah? Plenty more fish to catch, still yet."

It took about five hours.

It would have taken almost that long just to pull the line back up, even with no fish on it, because the pressure down there was so strong. Even for Sanji or Papa.

The sun had dropped below the bright gold horizon by the time Papa and Sanji reached over the side and hauled Billy's fish onto the boat—another yellowfin, almost twice the size of the one I caught. It was already dead, so Papa didn't have to club it.

But dead or not, Billy did it. And even though Papa and Sanji acted like they were irritated by missing out on more fishing, they let Billy finish the job. From the beginning they knew it would take that long.

"That's why you gotta stop the line," Papa said. Billy looked like he was about to pass out. Papa grinned and ruffled his hair. "Put 'um in the box."

When it was all over, and Billy's fish was squashing all the other fish in the fish box, Sanji reached out and shook Billy's hand. "How you feel, *haole* boy?"

"Like something Tomi's dog coughed up."

Sanji laughed and said, "If was me, I cut the damn line, already."

•   •   •

We laid sleeping mats out on the open deck, the *Taiyo Maru* rocking easily. Everyone was too tired to do any night fishing, so we decided to rest awhile.

Papa broke out Mama's *bento,* which means "lunch," and it was extra good, because we had Billy as our guest. *Musubi,* sticky rice wrapped in seaweed, with *ume* inside. *Ume,* which is the best part, is a small red pickled plum. So good when you finally reach it in the middle. Even Billy liked it. In fact he ate three of them. And Mama had also put in some *shoyu aku,* marinated to perfection. And to top it off, she made *tamagoyaki,* which is grilled egg shaped like little square cookies. Put all that together with the cool, fresh drinking water and you had a feast. Billy was converted. He said that after a roasting day of hard work it tasted like heaven itself. For me, I could see the *magokoro,* all the love and attention Mama put into making it for us. For a moment, I missed her.

The sea was quiet and smooth, with only long, slow swells moving under the boat. The deck smelled like fish and wet wood. Above, the night was loaded with stars, the dippers and planets that Mr. Ramos talked about in class.

Some of them blinked and looked like they were on fire, even with a three-quarter moon rising.

I drank about a gallon of water and fell asleep thinking about the universe, and wondering if anyone lived up there. Then I got to thinking about the pigeons and home and Lucky, and when she would have her puppies.

I woke up around three or four in the morning to the sound of mumbling voices. The stars had lost a lot of their brightness, and the night air was cooler. But the moon was so clear and white it looked fake. It shot a bright reflection across the ocean, like a bridge to the boat.

"Yeah, yeah," Sanji said. "I can see 'um. . . . Chee, I never knew had *mountains.*" He was sitting next to Billy on the fish box, studying the moon through Billy's binoculars. Papa was asleep near the deckhouse.

"Turn the eyepiece to focus it better," Billy said.

For a while, Sanji worked the eyepiece in silence. Then, still looking through the binoculars, he said, "You work hard today. . . . I thought you would only watch."

Billy didn't answer.

"Hey," Sanji went on, putting the binoculars down. "You know what? You the first *haole* I ever talk to in my life. . . . Can you believe that?"

"Really?" Billy said.

"No joke."

"How come?"

"I don't know. . . ." He paused a moment, then said, "I never went school like you and Tomi . . . just played around the boats until I was old enough to work. I learn to talk English from one Portagee I was working with at Tuna Packers.''

"Well, you're the first fisherman I've ever heard say he'd cut the line with a fish on it," Billy said.

Sanji laughed. "I guess that's the difference between Japanee and *haole*. I don't fish for fun."

"You call what I did fun?"

Sanji laughed again and slapped Billy on the back. "You okay—what you said your name was?"

"Billy."

"Oh, yeah, Billy . . . like billy goat."

"Yeah." Billy put his hands behind him on the fish box and leaned back.

Sanji picked up the binoculars again and raised them to the moon. He and Billy were two dark silhouettes against a silver sea.

"Chee," Sanji whispered, still amazed by the big white ball he saw through Billy's binoculars. "Chee."

The next day, on the way back to the island, we watched another fishing boat going out. It passed pretty close to us. You could see three men working around the deck. Billy waved at them, but they ignored him.

"They not going wave at you," Sanji said.

"Why not?"

"Hawaiian boat . . . they no like Japanee boat."

"Why?"

Sanji shook his head. "Before, had only Hawaiian boats. . . . Now got mostly Japanee boats . . . and a pretty crowded sea."

When the boat passed by, Papa stared straight ahead, toward the harbor. He didn't even glance at it.

• • •

Papa sold everything we caught, except for Billy's yellowfin, which me and Billy put between us in the back of
Sanji's truck. Papa covered it with a wet burlap bag to
keep it cool.

When we got up to our house, Billy and I dragged it
out of the truck, hauled it up the trail, and took it around
back by the water tank. We set it down on a patch of grass.
Billy wiped his hands on his pants and rubbed his arms.
"No way that thing's only a hundred fifty pounds."

"I know. Feels more like eight hundred."

Papa got his fish-cleaning knife from the kitchen and
made a long razor-thin slit along the belly, beginning just
behind the gills. The skin separated and guts started to
spill out onto the grass. Sanji squatted on his heels and
watched, waiting for a piece of tuna to take home.

"You take some fish, too, Billy," Sanji said. "Cook
'um with lemon."

The setting sun burned through the trees and
stretched long shadows across the yard. Everything that
wasn't in shadows was golden, even Lucky, who I had to
keep pushing away from the guts with my foot.

Papa was scraping out the stomach cavity when Keet
and his father showed up.

"Good evening, Wilson-sama," Papa said, quickly
standing. He bowed to Mr. Wilson, a smooth, polite ges-
ture, one arm wet to the elbow with fish slime and bits of
blood.

Mr. Wilson half-bowed back. "That's a mighty fine-looking yellowfin you got there, Taro."

"Unhhh," Papa grunted in agreement. "Billy got this one."

"No kidding," Keet said. "You really caught that, Billy?"

Billy nodded with his shy grin. "Yeah."

"Mighty fine, boy, mighty fine," Mr. Wilson said again, tapping Billy's shoulder. He shook his head in amazement, then said, "Well, the boy and I are just out for a walk around the property."

Keet and his father started to walk away. Sometimes Mr. Wilson was okay, but you never knew.

"Wait," Papa said. "Come. Take some fish. Good, this kind, you know. I cut you some."

Mr. Wilson turned back and raised his eyebrows. "Well, that would be damn nice of you, Taro."

Papa cut away a huge slab and handed it to me. "Take inside, Tomi. Rinse off and put inside rice bag."

I took it into the kitchen and washed it while Mama rummaged around for a rice bag. She found one and wrapped the meat neatly. I took it back out and handed it to Keet.

Keet reached for it with a slight smile, but averted his eyes. Maybe he was embarrassed for me to see him being like a nice person. "Thanks," he said.

"Sure."

Mr. Wilson put his hand on Keet's shoulder. "Let's go. Better get that in the icebox."

Keet nodded, then walked away backward, looking at me and Billy. He flicked his eyebrows and grinned. Billy waved and Keet turned, lifting the slab of fish to his shoulder on the palm of his hand.

Papa winked at Billy. "You nice to give away that fish."

"No problem," Billy said, and I laughed.

For a few days I actually thought Keet was okay. I could forget about the past and maybe we could even become friends again.

And then the spying started.

Black Zenith

The World Series began on the first day of October, not a minute too soon. Keet was getting on my nerves.

At first he'd started sneaking around, watching me out by the pigeons, and then, getting braver, he moved to the bushes around our house. One time, Grampa caught him nosing around the chickens and chased him away with a machete. Keet just laughed and called him a crazy old Buddhahead as he ran.

So I was more than ready to listen to the Yankees and the Dodgers. Anyway, fifteen very-hard-to-get cents were at stake. You could buy a new baseball for that!

I figured me and the Dodgers had a pretty good chance—Pete Reiser the slugger, Pee Wee Reese, and Mickey Owen the catcher. And Whit Wyatt, a twenty-two–game winner. Not bad.

But the Yankees had Joe DiMaggio, ace pitcher Red Ruffing, and Joe Gordon the slugger.

Grampa had a very good friend, an old goat with white hair named Charlie, the same Charlie who'd given Papa the opelu bait fish. Charlie was pure Hawaiian and worked for Billy's parents as their gardener. He lived on the Davises' place like we lived on the Wilsons', but Charlie's house was even smaller than ours.

Grampa and Charlie spent a lot of their spare time together. Mostly they just sat around and talked. But sometimes Grampa managed to talk Charlie into going down to Kaka'ako with him to watch Japanese silent movies, the kind where they had a *benshi,* the actor-guy who would give you the dialogue. Grampa loved those movies, especially when they had samurai ones.

Charlie was one of the nicest guys in the world. He'd never tell Grampa those movies were junk, even if he thought they were. He went along, though he probably couldn't understand more than about ten words of Japanese.

Anyway, Charlie had something that Grampa would have given half his chickens for—an old black Zenith radio that you could hear the police on. If Grampa loved anything, it was listening to the police talking to each other on that radio. Charlie and Grampa listened almost every night.

Billy and I managed to talk Charlie into letting us listen to the World Series on his Zenith. Who wanted to listen to it at Billy's house with Keet and Jake around?

I didn't know until we were sitting down to listen to the first game that Billy had already brainwashed Charlie over to the Yankees. In fact, Charlie couldn't wait for the games to start. Poor Grampa just scowled. He hated American baseball, because he couldn't understand what the radio said. Too fast. If he liked Japanese *yakyu,* the Japanese kind of baseball, he never said anything about it to me.

The first three games went very well . . . for Billy. He was already telling me how he was going to spend my fifteen cents. Okay, so what? Brooklyn was behind two games to one, but they could come back. They still had four games to go.

The day of the fourth game was a gray and stormy Sunday. Thunder rumbled around in the low clouds that sat heavily on the valley. Grampa had already gone over to Charlie's to listen to the police before the game started, but I had to boil water in the backyard and help Mama wash clothes.

Mama finally told me I was more trouble than I was worth and that I might as well get on over to Charlie's house before I drove her crazy.

I slipped on a sweatshirt and headed out into the trees. Lucky started to follow, but hurried back under the house when a big *crack* of thunder exploded in the sky.

I took the trail to diamond grass, and checked to make sure the wind hadn't blown off the two heavy tarps I'd put over the pigeon lofts.

The first fat raindrop thunked down on my shoulder just as I reached the trees on the other side. Then the clouds opened up, like a crane unloading a couple thousand fish into a truck. The rain swept over the jungle in a huge wave of thundering and hissing that came from every direction. I headed into it.

A popping sound caught my ear, a muffled echo in the dripping jungle. I stopped to listen and heard another one, then a voice, someone shouting over the roar of the rain. I crouched behind a tree.

"There . . . that tree . . . that's a Nazi."

Bam! A bullet thwacked into a tree a few feet away from me. I dropped down into the mud and covered my head with my arms.

"Maybe we should get out of this rain."

Jake.

"Don't be such a tilly," Keet said.

I peeked up and saw the two of them creeping past, crouching low like hunting soldiers, their shirts soaked and sticking to their backs. When they'd passed, I wiped the mud off my knees and ran the rest of the way.

A shiver snaked through me. I didn't know if it was from the rain or from almost getting shot.

Charlie's small house looked like an old umbrella with the rain rolling down the corrugated iron roof and pouring out of the rusty gutters around its edge. Water slapped down into big puddles below.

Billy saw me coming through the screen door and opened it as I ran up to the house. "Yuck," he said. "Looks like you fell in the mud."

I dragged off my soaked and muddy sweatshirt and squeezed the water out of it.

"Long time no see," Charlie said. "What you been up to?"

"Working, what else?"

Grampa humphed, glancing up at me from Charlie's old couch.

"Good," Charlie said. "Work is good. If you no work, bombye you go nuts." He smiled, his eyes crinkling at the edges.

"*. . . somewhere down Kalihi Street,*" a small, static-ridden voice coming out of the radio said. "*A lady complaining about a man sitting on top her roof . . .*"

Grampa leaned closer.

"*I'm on my way,*" another voice answered.

"*But Jimmy . . .*" the first one said.

"*What?*"

"*The guy naked. . . .*"

"*Must be nuts.*"

"*You want me to send a backup?*"

"*I'll let you know when I get there.*"

Grampa smiled at all that. But when he saw me looking at him, he frowned and dismissed me with a wave of his hand.

"When's the game come on?" I asked.

"I think it's on now," Billy said, giving me the you-tell-him look.

"Grampa, turn it to the game," I said.

"Wait, confonnit," Grampa growled. He turned up the static and leaned in over the radio, waiting for more about the man on the roof. I looked at Billy and shrugged.

Finally, Grampa grabbed his oiled paper umbrella, then went outside to the outhouse. It had to be coming down pretty hard for Grampa to use an umbrella.

As soon as he was out of the house, Billy and I jumped up and turned the dial around. Charlie chuckled.

We moved closer to listen.

"Get away from that," Grampa said, back too soon. He shook the rain off the umbrella before closing the screen door.

"Aw, come on, Grampa," I said. "This is an important game, and it's probably half over by now."

"Hummmph." Grampa came toward us, and me and Billy got out of the way, quick. Grampa sat back down on the couch and stared straight ahead. But he didn't change the radio back to the police. When I started to say thanks, he said, "Shhhh!"

Another blast of thunder boomed through the house and sent sputters of static out of the radio. *"Ka'a ka pohaku,"* Charlie said. "The stones roll." The rain *really* came down after that. Grampa turned the radio way up to hear it over the roar.

"I *love* this rain," Billy said.

I nodded. It *was* great.

They were in the fourth inning. The Dodgers had to win to keep their spirits up. Both teams had already used up two or three pitchers each. The score was three to nothing, Yankees, and Billy was practically prying the fifteen cents out of my pocket.

Then the Dodgers came up to bat in the bottom of the fourth and scored two runs. With the score still three to two in the fifth inning, the Dodgers' Dixie Walker hit to deep left for a double. After that, Pete Reiser slugged a fastball over the left field fence and the place went crazy. You could hear nothing but cheering for at least five minutes. I started to yell, too, but Grampa shot me a look. Actually, he looked a little worried.

"Fifteen cents," I said to Billy.

"I never give up on my team, *compadre*. . . . They'll be back. . . . You wait."

"That's right," Charlie said. "Yankees good. What you think, Joji-san?"

"Humph," Grampa mumbled. What a laugh to ask him anything.

Now the Dodgers were leading—four to three. And it stayed that way until the top of the ninth, when the Yankees got one last chance to do something.

The first two batters went down right away, two groundouts. Mickey Owen was catching. I could almost feel Casey's pitches pounding into Owen's glove, dust puffing out when they hit, like when Billy threw me fastballs on a hot day.

One out to go. One out for a Dodger win.

The Yankees' Tommy Henrich came up to bat and quickly racked up a full count, three balls and two strikes. Then came the last pitch.

Henrich swung . . . and missed!

The game was over. The fans went wild. The Dodgers had won!

Then the announcer screamed that the pitch Henrich struck out on had slipped through Mickey Owen's glove, and was rolling all the way back to the grandstand. *"The ball went right through Owen's glove!"* he yelled. "It's a *fair* ball! There goes Henrich!"

Owen ran back to get the loose ball.

The Dodger fans were roaring, still believing they'd won.

But the Yankees were still alive.

Henrich raced to first and beat Owen's throw. Charlie and Billy were so excited they jumped up and down like lunatics. Grampa gawked up at them.

The announcer was hoarse. The people at the game didn't know what to do, he said. Some of them had already run out onto the field. "Oh my," the announcer said. "Oh my, oh my, oh my."

Criminy, I wished Billy and I were there to see it.

It took a few minutes to get the fans back into the stands. So now, the Yankees had Henrich on first and Joe DiMaggio coming up to bat. *"Just one out,"* I pleaded, lacing my fingers together and squeezing my palms until my hands turned white. I held my breath.

Tock!

DiMaggio singled.

I bit my fingers. Billy slapped my back. "You watch," he said.

Keller, next to bat, doubled. Henrich and DiMaggio scored, and Billy was all over the place. Grampa got up and moved out of the way into the safety of Charlie's kitchen.

"Casey's rattled," Billy whooped.

"Take him out," I yelled, as if they could hear me. But they let him keep pitching.

The Yankees finally ended up winning, seven to four. And the Dodgers' spirit was broken—not to mention mine, because I knew Billy would never let me forget it.

After the game Grampa came back and tuned the

Zenith to the police, then sat there shaking his head. I think he decided that we were all very, very strange.

• • •

It was pitch-black by the time we finally got up to leave. The rain was still pouring down like crazy. Grampa nodded to Charlie and headed out the door, popping up the umbrella. Raindrops thundered down on it.

Billy and I made plans to listen to the next game, but I was feeling pretty low. Billy tapped the side of my arm and sprinted out into the rain. I pulled my damp sweatshirt over my head and said good-bye to Charlie.

Outside, the trees swayed and shivered, leaves *whooshing* down. The whole place smelled sharp, like rusting iron. Where was Keet? Even he wasn't stupid enough to still be stalking around in the jungle . . . was he? It was lucky he only had his .22 and not his father's .45. The .22 would just make a small hole, but the .45 would take your head off.

Grampa's pale ghost of an umbrella moved up and down as he strode deeper into the darkness ahead of me. I tried to forget about Keet and think about Grampa. I thought about how he came to join Papa in Hawaii after Grandma had died.

He came here to be a fisherman, like Papa had long before I was born. Grampa still had his old purple-colored passport hidden safely under Grandma's altar. He was proud of that purple color. Back in the olden days they had two kinds, purple and green: green for contract workers, who had to work and then go home, and purple was for the guys who came with their own businesses and skills, and could stay in the islands. Grampa's business was boats and fishing.

I wondered if even now Grampa still needed his passport because he wasn't allowed to be an American citizen. I was, because I was born here. But the law wouldn't allow Grampa. Or Mama and Papa. Papa said the *haoles* wanted Japanese to come work, but not stay around afterward. But most people did stay.

In Japan, Papa told me, Grampa was very well respected. He had a lot of friends. But he missed Papa and came to the islands. When he got here he was pretty lonely and hardly spoke to anyone, even to Papa. Then he met Charlie and went back to his old self. Grampa learned to speak English from Charlie.

You had to love that old man. He did what he wanted, no matter what. And he didn't always back away from trouble, like Papa wanted me to do. If Grampa had been me, he would have busted Keet Wilson's nose already. I was sure of it.

Thunder on
the Moon

Toward the end of October something very strange happened. Billy and I had gotten off the bus after school and were walking up to our street. When we got there we saw a brand-new car, a blue Cadillac, waiting to turn out onto the main road.

"Whose car is that?"

"I don't know," Billy said, "but it must have cost a couple of bucks."

"You can say that again."

"I don't know, but it must have cost a couple of bucks."

"Shuddup," I said, poking him with my elbow.

When we got closer, I saw that the driver was Mr. Wilson. Billy and I both waved, but Mr. Wilson just glared at us, giving us the worst stink eye I'd seen since we beat the Kaka'ako Boys.

"What's *his* problem?" I whispered to Billy.

"Who knows?"

I turned away as we walked past. It was so strange. He'd never been like that to us before. When I couldn't stand it anymore, I glanced back to see if he was still looking at us. He was. You could see his eyes in the rear-view mirror.

"He's still looking," I said.

Billy turned to see for himself.

We started walking again.

Just then the car's tires squealed. Billy and I spun around and saw the Cadillac backing up, coming toward us fast. We jumped out of the way as the car slid to a stop. Mr. Wilson leaned over and rolled down the window.

"Come here," he said.

Billy and I stood there gaping at him. I thought he wanted Billy, because Mr. Wilson hardly ever said a word to me.

"You," Mr. Wilson said, pointing his finger at me.

"Me?" I stepped closer to the window and leaned down. Mr. Wilson glared back at me. His neck sagged over the collar of his starched white shirt.

"Listen to this, boy," he said in a low voice. "You people are walking on mighty thin ice around here." I didn't even breathe. For a moment, he wagged his finger at me without saying anything. Then, in almost a whisper, he said, "You tell your father I don't want to see any more of that Jap crap around my place . . . you understand?"

I nodded.

Mr. Wilson stepped on the gas. The car spit dust and little rocks out when it took off.

"What did he want?" Billy asked.

My hands started to tremble. "I don't know. . . . I better go home."

I hurried down the road toward my house with Billy running to keep up. *Jap crap?* What did Mr. Wilson mean?

•   •   •

We ran up the trail, through the trees, and burst out into the open. No one in sight. What was Mr. Wilson *talking* about?

Lucky barked. Up by the chickens. Billy and I took off toward the commotion.

Kimi, jumping up and down and clapping her hands, was watching Grampa standing there slowly waving his giant flag back and forth, back and forth. He'd tied the ends to a long pole, and at the top of his lungs was singing *"Kimigayo,"* the Japanese national anthem, the slowest song in the history of the world. And tied around his shiny cannonball head he had another white piece of cloth.

"Grampa! What are you *doing?*"

Grampa stopped singing and glared at me, looking me over from head to foot, scornfully, like he was considering how to slice me in half. Then he started singing again.

"Grampa, Mr. Wilson heard you, and saw that flag. He yelled at me and said he didn't want to see any more of that . . . of that . . . of that stuff around his place. You gotta stop!"

Grampa cut his singing off in the middle of a word and walked toward me in that boastful way the movie samurais do. He stopped right in front of my face.

"Ojii-chan," I said, much more softly, more respectfully. "Mr. Wilson . . . please . . . Mr. Wilson saw you and he's very mad. I know it sounds stupid, but he said he didn't want to see any Japanese stuff around here."

Grampa's eyes were icy under the white headband, which was made of two old handkerchiefs tied together. Billy stood off to the side, his eyes about to pop out of his head.

"We are *Japanese,* confonnit. . . . *Japanese!"* Grampa looked at me like it was all *my* fault. Then he flicked Kimi a quick wave with his chin and started back toward the house. Kimi followed, refusing to look at me.

Mr. Wilson's angry eyes were still scaring me half to death. But Grampa's song was only part of it. Mama had the rest of the story when she got home from work. She brought the Wilsons' thrown-away newspaper for me to read to her. She could read Japanese, but not English. Whatever was on the front page, she said, it made Mr. Wilson very angry.

I sat down at the kitchen table and spread the paper out in front of me. "The Germans sunk one of our ships," I said.

Mr. Ramos had told us about the sinking in school, but I was only half listening. I hadn't realized it was an *American* ship.

"Read," Mama said, the look on her face flat.

U.S. DESTROYER IS SUNK BY TORPEDO OFF ICELAND

Washington, Friday, Oct. 31. (UP) The Navy Department announced today that the destroyer USS *Reuben James* was sunk last night by a torpedo west of Iceland.

No further details are available at present.

In a photograph just below the headline, the *Reuben James* sat peacefully in a glassy harbor. The sailors were dressed in white and lined up on the deck. Below the photo it said FIRST U.S. WARSHIP SUNK.

Mama stood there with her arms crossed, looking out the window. Finally, she went over and opened the back door and called for Kimi to come inside.

• • •

Very early the next morning, before the sun came up, Lucky started barking under the house. I could hear her through the floorboards beneath my bed.

Grampa sat up on his mat.

"Something's wrong with Lucky," I said. I couldn't find the lantern, so I just grabbed a box of matches and ran down the back steps.

It was too dark to see, but I knew where Lucky slept. She heard me crawling toward her and whined between barks. When I got close, I took a match out and struck it. Three sets of small red eyes froze and stared back at me.

Mongooses.

"Ghaaaaa!" I said, and they scurried away.

The match went out and I lit another one. Why were mongooses bothering Lucky? I crawled closer.

"Lucky . . . you little rabbit."

Four squirmy pups nudged at her belly. Actually, they were more like four wet blobs. They must have just come out, or else Lucky had licked them. I'd never seen puppies so new.

Grampa crawled up beside me.

"The mongooses were trying to get at them," I said.

"Uhnnn."

The puppies looked like they were born too early, their ears nothing but furry tabs. They looked more like rats than dogs. "Is there something wrong with them?"

"Nah," Grampa said. "They born blind . . . and deaf . . . but pretty soon eye come right, and ear."

"Got to build a fence, or something," I said. "To protect them."

Grampa studied Lucky's puppies a moment, his face soft and hard at the same time. He wasn't very interested in animals as pets, but he was soft on any kind of babies. He even felt like that for baby chicks, even when he knew they would soon grow to be as cranky as he was.

Grampa and I watched the puppies fumble around Lucky's belly, trying to drink. Then we crawled out from under the house. The sky had changed, just barely, going from black to purple. Grampa's rooster started to crow.

Mama must have heard Lucky's barking too. The light from the kitchen window spilled out over the grass. The cool scent of ginger from the jungle filled the air as Grampa and I clomped up the wooden steps.

"Lucky had puppies," I told Mama. The screen door slapped behind me and Mama scowled. She hated loud noises like that. "Sorry," I said.

Kimi was sitting at the kitchen table. "I want to see," she said.

"Later," Mama said. "Too dark now."

"You got any extra chicken wire?" I asked Grampa. "I need to make a fence."

"No need fence," he said. "No need dogs, confonnit. Take 'um on the boat . . . drown 'um."

I turned to Mama, and she raised her eyebrows. "Who can pay to feed dogs?"

"I can ask the Wilsons for scraps, or the Davises. . . . I can get it. . . ."

Mama studied me, considering it. "If you can feed 'um, you can keep 'um. But when they get little bit more old, you can only keep one. Give away the rest."

"Okay, okay."

"Who going drown them, anyway?" Mama said. "Not you. Not me, for goodness sakes. And not that poor old man sitting there looking mean."

Grampa humphed, then got up to go light some incense at the *butsudan.* And probably to consult Grandma about what should be done about Lucky's puppies.

When I came home from school later that day, I hurried under the house and found a perfectly squared chicken-wire fence around Lucky and her pups. It even had a gate to let Lucky in and out.

"Grampa," I said, when I found him and Kimi out by the chickens. "Who built that fence? Did *you* do that?"

"Was my dogs, I drown 'um, you can bet."

I smiled. He was such a bad liar. "Thanks, Grampa."

"Watch out the damn mongoose," he said, pushing past me, bumping my arm.

• • •

Billy came over later and stayed under our house practically all afternoon looking at Lucky's pups. He went home and came back after dark to look some more.

"That one is Red," he finally said, touching a pale tan one with a white saddle on it. Lucky got nervous and growled a little. Billy moved his hand away and Lucky looked up at him with forgiving eyes. The puppy twitched in its sleep, the light from the lantern warm and yellow.

"How come that one?"

"It's the smallest."

"Red Ruffing isn't small."

"Yeah, but Red Ruffing would pick the small one if he was picking. . . . How could he help it? The small one needs you the most."

I shrugged. "Okay, it's yours."

"What is it, anyway?" Billy asked. "Boy or girl?"

"I don't know. Take a look under its tail and see."

"What do you look for?" Billy said.

"How should I know? Just look and see what you can see."

Billy picked up the puppy and lifted the tail. Then he looked under the tails of the rest of the pups. "They all look the same."

"All girls? Or boys?"

"I don't know," Billy said.

"Can't you tell a boy from a girl?"

"You try, then."

So I studied them carefully. Billy was right. "Well, anyway," I said, "it's your dog. Boy or girl."

We finally got back out from under the house. Billy had to get home. I walked with him as far as diamond grass. We couldn't stop talking about Lucky's puppies. I was going to train one to shake hands, and Billy was going to teach Red to catch tennis balls.

"Good luck," I said. "If Red is anything like Lucky, all he's going to do is sleep and chew those balls to rags."

Just then, the night sky exploded into rays of light. Searchlights. The mountains behind us looked flat and close in the beams that crawled along the ridges.

Billy read my mind. We took off for the banyan tree, stumbling through the ghostly jungle half-lit by the glowing clouds. I followed Billy up the massive trunk into the branches. We clawed our way to the top, where there was an opening in the leaves. My legs felt rubbery, I'd climbed so fast.

"Holy moly," Billy said, gawking out toward the horizon. From where we were you could see the whole side of the island and miles and miles of ocean. There must have been fifty searchlights, some shining into the sky, some running along the mountains, and some blasting out to sea, scanning the water.

"Maneuvers," Billy said.

"Yeah . . . incredible."

Long, straight beams of blue-white light crisscrossed each other, back and forth, slicing through the black night. And far out on the ocean, you could see dots of ships caught like roaches in the powerful beams.

A breeze whisked up from the town below, bringing

with it the night smell of seawater and honeysuckle mixed together. I leaned closer to the branch, gripping it tighter, its sandpapery bark pinching my palms.

Then the lights went out.

The island turned black. Only small yellow lights from the city sparkled below, like distant campfires. Far away in the hills on the west end of the island, red flashes flickered in the sky, followed seconds later by rumbling sounds, like thunder on the moon.

"Those army guys never stop," Billy said.

Night maneuvers. I listened to the eerie, muffled explosions. Strange. Kind of scary . . . like it was all happening in outer space somewhere.

I lay awake for more than an hour that night. You hardly ever thought about the army, and then you were suddenly reminded it was still there, like somebody's grumpy watchdog. I kept seeing the boats caught in the searchlights out on the horizon. Maybe one of them was Papa's. I tried to put myself out there, out on the *Taiyo Maru*, looking back at those blasts of light. The boat was so small, just a leaf on the sea. A plane could bomb it out of the water in a second.

•   •   •

When Papa came home early the next morning, I showed him the story about the *Reuben James*. He sat down at the kitchen table and studied the picture. Grampa was next to the window, sitting as straight as a stop sign.

Papa couldn't read English either, so he handed the paper back and asked me to read it to him.

"What does it mean, Papa?" I asked, when I'd finished.

Lines of worry stood between his eyes. "Hard to say, Tomi . . ."

But I knew what he worried about—the Japanese, who were making war with China and arguing with the U.S. about it, making war like the Germans were. And though the U.S. wasn't at war with anyone, maybe it was only a matter of time until it would be.

"Lot of people in Honolulu starting to point finger," Papa said. "They wondering whose side us Hawaii-Japanee going take, and what we going do if Japan and U.S. got into a fight."

Maybe that was what Mr. Wilson was wondering too.

For a few minutes no one spoke. I felt kind of queasy. Under the house Lucky barked, and made me jump. I watched Papa study the picture of the *Reuben James*. Had the men on it drowned, or gotten blown up? I wanted to ask Papa if he'd seen the searchlights, and I wanted to tell him about Mr. Wilson, and what he'd said. And I hadn't even told him about Lucky's puppies.

But I didn't say a word.

9

The Butcher

"**Gentlemen . . .** and I use that term loosely," Mr. Ramos said. "Remember the science project? Well, this is it. The deadline for telling me what you will be working on."

I glanced over at Billy and Mose and Rico. For once, the three of them were sitting up straight and looking as innocent as Lucky's puppies.

Mr. Ramos sat on the edge of his desk. "Well?" he said.

Billy raised his hand.

"Ah, Billy. Good. What's it going to be?"

"I thought I would make a display on how to throw a curveball. I could do some drawings and write something. And then I could do a demonstration."

Mr. Ramos raised his eyebrows. "Hmmm . . . more

like physics than earth science. But if that's what you want to do, then that will be fine."

Mose and Rico stared at their desks.

"Okay, the Corteles cousins . . . what about you?"

"Mose and I want to do one together," Rico said.

Mose perked up.

"Let's hear it, then," Mr. Ramos said.

"We're going to make a vollacano and show how it works."

Mose stared at Rico. I had to laugh, it was so obvious Mose hadn't heard a thing about any volcano project.

"All right," Mr. Ramos said. "But first you've got to get the pronunciation right. It's *volcano*. And it better be good, because there will be two of you working on one project. . . . Understand?"

"Yessir, Mr. Ramos," Rico said.

Mose nodded okay.

Billy put his hand up to cover his mouth and whispered to Rico, "Yessir, Mr. Ramos." Rico reached across the aisle and slapped Billy's arm with the back of his hand.

"Was there something else, Rico?" Mr. Ramos asked.

"No, no. That's all."

"Okay. Now, this is for all of you. I want to see some *real* progress by December fifteenth—that's one month from now."

Mr. Ramos winked at Mose and Rico, but Mose didn't see it. He was too busy writing a note to Rico.

• • •

After school, we skipped the school bus and headed out to catch a city bus. Rico had heard a rumor that the Kaka'ako Boys had a new pitcher, who was also a slugger, some guy from the island of Hawaii who was over six feet tall . . . and only in the eighth grade. We had to check it out.

Mose was still in a bad mood over the volcano. But for Rico, the more he thought about it, the more he slapped himself on the back. "Don't worry," he said to Mose. "Easy, this. All we gotta do is get a pile of mud and dig a hole in the middle. Then let it dry and paint some red coming out. Maybe put a stink bomb inside to make it smell like real."

"Jeese." Mose rolled his eyes. "This is a *science* project. You gotta do a report, and you gotta be able to *explain* the thing. Who's gonna do that?"

"You. I make it, you fake it."

Mose shoved Rico. "Do me a favor—don't think anymore today, okay?"

"Here comes the bus," I said. "Stop goofing off, or he won't let us on."

Mose and Rico settled down. The driver gave us dirty looks when we put our five cents in the meter. We stumbled to the back while the bus lurched on down the hill toward the ocean.

"Rico, how much money you got left?"

"Nothing."

Mose looked at me. "That was all I had."

We all turned to Billy.

"Rich *haole*," Rico said. "It's up to you, or else we going walk back."

"Ten cents," Billy said.

"I told you he was rich," Rico said.

"But not rich enough," I added. "Two of us gotta walk."

"Nah," Billy said. "We can all walk."

Mose shook his head and started another round of shoving. But we stopped when we noticed the bus driver's eyes in the mirror.

We got off and headed down to Atkinson Park, where they had a couple of baseball diamonds. We passed the soda works and the soy factory, the buildings squeezed so close together only a cock-a-roach could fit between them. Small kids were playing in the streets. They were a mixed-up bunch of all the races in Kaka'ako, mostly boys who roamed around like ants. A bunch of them followed us in a pack about a block behind.

That part of Kaka'ako was crammed with falling-down two-story wooden buildings with laundry hanging from every window. I loved that place. I'd been down there on Japanese festival days with my family, and many times with Papa to see his fishermen friends. Once in a while I even went with Mama and Kimi to visit Mama's old picture-bride acquaintances.

As we walked Billy got quiet, like he was trying to hide. I couldn't blame him. You didn't see many *haoles* down there. Everyone noticed him, with his blond hair and baby-pink face.

Ahead of us seven boys, all Japanese, hung around blocking the way to the park. We had to walk through them or else cross the street like cowards. But Rico and Mose weren't about to cross any street for anybody.

"Now we've had it," I whispered.

"What, from those punks?" Rico pulled a stick match out of his pocket and stuck it in his mouth like a toothpick.

We kept walking, Rico strutting ahead. The gang slowly bunched up, but Rico kept on going straight at them. If a fight broke out I'd yell *"Police, police,"* and hope they'd run for it.

Rico moved up, nose to nose with the biggest guy, except that Rico's nose was only at the guy's chin. But Rico just stood there with the stick match almost touching the big guy's neck. Nobody said a word. Seven boys giving us deadly looks.

Rico pushed on past, then turned and looked back with his hands on his hips, waiting for me and Mose and Billy.

Mose turned sideways and bumped his way through. Then me, so close I could smell the oil on the guy's hair and see the small pin-sized pimples on his chin.

But when Billy tried to pass, the big guy stepped in front of him.

Billy started over to the other side of the street. One of the smaller guys followed in front of him, blocking his way step for step.

Billy stopped and looked over at us. The guy kept staring at him, about two inches from his face. But Billy ignored him. He wasn't afraid. He just didn't like trouble.

The big guy came up to me. "How come you bring these *haoles* down this place?"

Rico pushed me out of the way. He spit the stick match out of his mouth. "Who you calling one *haole?*"

The big guy nodded his head toward Billy. "The lily-white punk over there . . . and you, too, in fack . . . yeah, you." He put his fingertips on Rico's chest and pushed him back.

Bok!

Rico landed one good punch. The big guy fell to the ground.

"Hey!" someone up the street yelled. "Hold it!"

A guy ran up to us, a man with a ballahead army-kind haircut. He was short, but he had big muscles. "Beat it," he said to the gang guys. "We don't need no trouble around here."

The big guy scrambled up, covering his eye. He seemed to know the ballahead man. He glared at Rico, then backed away. The rest of his gang looked at us like they wanted to tear our heads off. Finally they turned and disappeared into an alley.

"No worry about them," the man said. "They won't bother you if I'm around. They dumb, but they not stupit." He glanced over at Billy and smiled. "Hey . . . I know you. You the pitcher, yeah? Hoo, man, you good. What's your name?"

"Billy."

The man glanced at the rest of us. "I seen you guys too. You the team play my kid brother. Herbie Okubo . . . you know him? The kid play second base?"

"Oh, yeah," Mose said. "He's pretty good."

The man shook his head. "The bugga work hard.

. . . I never seen a kid practice like that. So, what you boys doing down Kaka'ako?"

"We heard they got a new pitcher," Billy said.

"Yeah," Rico added. "We heard he was six feet, maybe seven."

"Maybe eight. That's all Herbie been talking about for the last week," the man said, shaking his head. "How's about I come with you? I never seen him yet either."

"Sure," Mose said.

The man put his arm on Billy's shoulder. "Come on, *haole*. You welcome in this neighborhood. No worry about those punks. They always like that. Hell, I used to be like that myself. . . . No mean nothing, they just like to ack tough."

Billy nodded, and we headed into Atkinson Park. Some of the Kaka'ako Boys saw us coming and stopped fielding grounders that Hamamoto, the catcher, was hitting out to them. Soon they were all standing there staring at us.

"Hey, Herbie," the man said, waving to his brother. "No stop for us, we just like watch."

Herbie shrugged and punched his glove. Soon the Kaka'ako Boys forgot we were even there.

Except for when they called in their new pitcher.

He was way out in the outfield. He jogged in slowly, like one of those water buffaloes in Kailua. He wasn't Japanese like the others. He was some kind of mixture— maybe Japanese-Hawaiian-Portagee-Filipino.

He glanced over at us, looking mean, with his hair

greased straight back and muscles bulging out like boulders. He even had a shadow of a mustache.

"Holy smokes," Mose whispered.

"He looks like twelfth grade, already," Rico said. "Must be stupit, spent a lot of time flunking."

Ichiro Fujita, the Kaka'ako first baseman, smiled over at Billy. "Hey, *haole,* meet the Butcher." He laughed, and so did the rest of his team. "This guy not very patient," Ichiro went on. "We call him the Butcher . . . pretty soon you going fine out why."

"The guy look dumb as a rock," Rico whispered.

"Shhh," I said. "You want him to eat you for lunch, or what?"

"No worry," Rico said. "I think the guy eats dog food."

We all had to work hard to keep from laughing. The Butcher took a step toward us, and we shut up.

The Kaka'ako Boys came in and got ready to practice batting. And the Butcher started pitching.

He could throw the ball almost as fast as a bullet. What scared me the most was that he wasn't always on target. When the Kaka'ako Boys came up to bat, they stood about ten feet away from the plate and didn't take their eyes off the Butcher even for one second.

"Criminy," Mose said. "He could take your head off with one wild pitch."

"He could fix that," Billy said. "Look at the way he closes his eyes just as he lets the ball go. I could show him how to get better aim."

"No, no," Rico said. "No show him nothing. More

better to take a chance on getting hit than to help that babooze strike us out.''

The ballahead man got a kick out of that. "But if he crack your head, you might change your mind.''

"He crack my head, I crack his.''

"If you got a head left.''

"Listen,'' Rico said. "You come down this field January one, New Year's Day. . . . We got a rematch with these guys, and we ain't going to lose to no Frankenstein from the Big Island.''

"Okay, okay, no get hot. . . . I'll see if I can make it. . . . But do me a favor, yeah? Next time, come down South Street so those centipede boys don't bother you. Coral Street—where you came down? They think they own it.'' He shook hands with all of us. "Good luck, you kids. And don't forget what I told you, yeah?''

When we left Kaka'ako, Billy and I went down Pohukaina and headed up South, like the guy said. But Rico and Mose went strutting back up Coral with a pack of kids tailing them, like they were following a couple of lions in a circus parade.

===(10)===

Sunrise at Diamond Grass

On a Saturday, a few weeks after Billy, me, Mose, and Rico met the Butcher, I heard a gunshot. It was mid-afternoon, and I was helping Grampa with the chickens. He'd just handed me a can of eggs that he wanted me to take over to Mrs. Wilson.

Grampa and I turned toward the trees where the sound had come from.

Keet. Playing with his .22 again.

Grampa shook his head. There was another shot, and Grampa winced. He nodded toward the eggs. "Take 'um," he said.

"Aw, come on, Grampa . . . I don't want to go over there. . . ."

"Just take 'um." Grampa raised his hand like he was going to slap my head.

"Okay, okay."

Lucky followed me through the trees, sniffing around stumps and patches of weeds. Spots of sunlight speckled the trail.

When Lucky trotted out onto the Wilsons' lawn, Keet's dog went into a barking frenzy. He did that every single time I went over there.

"Rufus," I said, holding out my hand. He settled down and came over to sniff at Lucky, who kept turning around in circles.

The Wilsons had a screened-in back porch almost as big as our whole house. I knocked, then waited. Mr. Wilson's new Cadillac was parked in the driveway. I cringed when I saw what looked like a bullet hole in the back window. Keet and his stupid rifle. I prayed for anyone but Mr. Wilson to come to the door.

But no one came.

I put my hand up to the screen and peeked inside.

The door squeaked as I inched it open and walked in, creeping past the white-cushioned lounging chairs. I knocked on the kitchen door. No one answered, but I could hear voices. I inched the door open and put the eggs inside.

"You stupid idiot!" I heard Mr. Wilson shout.

"I told you, it was an *accident*," Keet said, his voice cracking.

A door slammed.

"Okay," Keet said. "I'll *pay* for the stupid window."

"Don't get sassy with me, young man, or I'll knock your block off."

"What do you—"

"Shut up! Give me that rifle."

"No!"

I heard a thud and something falling over. I imagined Keet struggling with his father, tugging the .22 back and forth. Keet started whining and sobbing, trying to talk. Crying like a baby.

His sobs got louder, closer. I started to back away.

"Get out of here," Mr. Wilson screamed. "I don't want to look at your stupid idiot face."

I left the eggs on the floor and ran out, sprinting across the grass toward the trees. Lucky and Rufus ran after me. I dove into the bushes, trying to hide.

Seconds later, Keet came bursting out. The screen door slapped back against the house with a loud *thwack!* He headed across the yard, coming right at me, wiping his eyes with his arm. I crouched as low in the bushes as I could get, digging down into the dirt, holding Lucky next to me. Rufus started nosing into my hiding place, thinking it was a game. I pushed him away with my foot, but he kept coming back.

The earth shook when Keet stomped by, slapping bushes from his path. He saw Rufus and kicked him. Rufus yelped and took off.

I held my breath and listened to the clink of Keet's dog tags fade away. I stayed hidden until I couldn't hear them anymore. The only sound was Lucky panting, hot in my ear. I felt sick. The ugliness in Mr. Wilson's voice was meaner by far than anything Keet had ever even tried to aim at me.

• • •

"Next time, you're taking those eggs over there your-self," I told Grampa.

He waved me off.

I gave Grampa a small shove on his arm. "I mean it, Grampa. That's it, I tell you."

He grinned, just a little.

"You think it's funny I had to go over there?" I reached out to shove him again.

Grampa grabbed my wrist, his grip as strong as an iron vise.

I hit the dirt before I could even figure out what had happened. Grampa let go and walked away. I sat there rubbing my wrist. "I mean it. I'm *never* going up there again," I said.

But Grampa just walked over to his creaky old bicycle and rode off to the silent movies in Kaka'ako, leaving me and Lucky to watch Kimi.

"That's the last time!" I shouted.

Kimi sat on the back steps watching me, looking lonely. It was hard on her, living so far away from any other girls her age. Her best friend lived downtown near the harbor. I took a deep breath, then let the air out slowly. "Hey," I said. "You want to see the puppies?"

She jumped up and hopped down the stairs with her feet together. *Thunk . . . thunk . . . thunk . . . thunk.*

"Maybe we can make up some names for them," I said.

"Azuki Bean," Kimi said.

"What?"

"Azuki Bean."

"Azuki bean?"

Kimi pointed under the porch.

With Lucky anxiously leading the way, we crawled under the house and went into the chicken-wire pen. The pups were almost a month old now. They got up and stumbled around. They poked at my hand with their wet noses and made tiny pinprick bites on my finger.

"Azuki Bean," Kimi said, stroking one of the pups—a runty-looking one, but not the one Billy wanted, thank goodness. How come everybody liked the small ones?

"That's what you want to name this one?"

Kimi nodded.

"Okay . . . Azuki Bean, then. What about the other ones?"

Kimi looked at them but didn't answer. She seemed to have no interest in the rest. Where did she get *that* name? Azuki beans were small, pebblelike beans.

After playing around with the puppies awhile I began to forget about the Wilsons' house. I also managed to forget to let the pigeons out, which I was supposed to do every afternoon. It was after dark when I finally remembered, but Papa said never to fly them at night, so I had to wait until morning, which broke their routine. All because of Keet Wilson. Or Grampa . . . yeah, Grampa.

"I promise you I'm not going over there again," I whispered to Grampa that night in the dark. He pretended to be sleeping, but I could tell he was awake because of how he breathed.

A mosquito hummed in my ear and I slapped it away.

• • •

As usual on Sunday mornings, Billy met me at diamond grass just after the sun came up. The field was still wet with dew, and in the brilliant sun, the whole place was alive with sparkles.

Billy brought his bat this time. "We can hit pop flies," he said. "All day, if we want. . . . My parents spent last night at the Royal Hawaiian Hotel for their anniversary."

"You stayed home by yourself?"

"No. Jake was there, and Keet. He came over yesterday. . . . Boy, was *he* in a bad mood. Come on, let's hit some balls."

"I have to let the birds out first. I forgot yesterday."

Flight and food went together, always. The birds, Papa drilled into me, needed to fly, and they needed to come back. To make that happen, he said, "Feed 'um right when they come home. . . . So they know. . . . So they have a good reason to come back."

The racers had gone an extra twelve hours without food and were pretty antsy. But they flew out anyway, batting by me, leaving puffs of feathery dust behind. In less than a minute they were out of sight beyond the trees.

I fed the other birds, put feed out for the racers, and told myself that one day without exercise wasn't going to hurt any of them.

"Okay, let's go," I said to Billy, then jogged out to the other side of the field and waited for him to hit me a ball. It was still early, not even eight o'clock.

"Hey," Billy called. "When are you going to pay up the fifteen cents?"

"Oh, yeah . . . I forgot."

"I should charge interest."

"Yeah, yeah, I know."

Tock.

Billy hit a high fly ball. I caught it and threw it back. Billy knocked it down with the end of the bat and picked it up. "I'll tell you what. You can give me five cents now and—"

Billy suddenly fell silent. Looked up.

"What?" I said, following his gaze.

"Listen."

Far away, you could hear explosions. It sounded like the time Mr. Davis drove us out to Schofield Barracks and we heard the army shooting in the hills.

"What is it?" I said.

Crummmp. Like thunder, far away. Then a droning of engines.

Crummp . . . thoomp, thoomp . . . thoomp.

An ear-shattering roar suddenly thundered down on us, a plane flying way too low. A dark fighter. It blasted over the trees. I ducked, and covered my head with my glove.

"Jeeze!" I said.

Billy just stood there gawking, his hand shading his eyes. The plane passed so close that its wake sent a shiver through the treetops. I covered my ears and watched it bank to the right. The cockpit windows flashed in the sun like mirrors. The fighter dropped lower and headed off toward the west end of the island.

"The banyan tree!" Billy said.

I tore off my glove and raced across the field after him. Another plane ripped over us. More planes droned and whined, farther away.

Crummmp . . . thoomp, thoomp.

Tat-tat-tat-tat-tat.

My heart began pounding. I raced into the trees after Billy, nearly blinded by snapping branches. We clawed our way up the tree. When we reached the top, another plane flew past, barely higher than the trees. Billy and I waved, but the pilot didn't notice us. What was going on? They *never* flew that low.

Huge, awful black clouds of smoke rolled up into the sky from Pearl Harbor. You could barely see the ships, which were lined up in neat rows like chips of gray metal. The smoke was so thick you couldn't even see the mountains. Hundreds of planes circled the sky like black gnats, peeling off and dropping down to vanish into the boiling smoke, then reappearing, shooting skyward with engines groaning, circling back, sunlight flashing when they turned.

"My *God,*" Billy whispered. "That smoke . . . it's . . . *ack-ack!* . . . This is for *real!*"

Crummmp.

Explosions of seawater burst skyward in the harbor. A plane crashed in the cane fields and started a fire. Another fell into the sea, spinning like a windmill with smoke trailing off it.

Tat-tat-tat-tat-tat

Thoomp . . . thoomp . . .

Another dark plane charged down on us from behind, screaming out of the valley from the mountains. Billy and I turned just as it boomed over, heading down toward the sea. The noise stabbed into my ears. The fighter banked abruptly, then sped back toward the swarm of planes circling Pearl Harbor.

Billy and I gaped at the pilot. He was so close you could see a white band around his head. Then it hit me. *Dark* plane. Not silver. Not a navy plane. It didn't even have a star on it.

It was amber. *All* the planes were amber.

A rush of fear swept over me.

Amber.

Amber, with a blood-red sun on the fuselage and under the wings . . . blood-red sun . . . the symbol of Japan.

The plane raced into a sky thick with black smoke.

A huge explosion shook the earth. Close. *Real* close. Black smoke tumbled skyward from down by the grocery store, where the school bus let us off. An ugly cloud rose like a monster out of the trees.

"Oh my God, oh my God," Billy said.

I couldn't take my eyes off the rising cloud of smoke. Couldn't think. Couldn't breathe.

"Come on!" Billy said, grabbing my arm.

My hands shook as I dropped from branch to branch, slipping, scraping my chest, my stomach, retreating into the darkness of the jungle. We hit the ground and stumbled out into the field.

Billy ran around in circles, jumping up and down, not knowing what to do.

Grampa burst out of the bushes, running into the field with his Japanese flag. I'd never seen him move so fast. He stopped and squinted up at the sky.

An amber fighter came up from the ocean and banked into a sweeping turn above the ridge. It headed back over us, back toward Pearl Harbor, dropping low as it approached. Grampa frantically flapped the flag. Up and down, up and down. The pilot wagged the wings of his plane, then sped past. The sound of the engine shattered the air.

"Grampa!" I yelled. "What are you *doing!*"

"He no bomb, he no bomb," Grampa said, his eyes filled with terror. "He see flag, he no bomb."

"No, no, no, Grampa! Put that thing away! Hide it! Hide!" I put my arm around his shoulder. It felt funny to do that, but he looked so terrified. "Come, *ojii-chan.* Let's go back. Quick, before another plane comes."

Grampa gave me a bewildered look. I urged him toward the trees, away from the open space. He dropped the flag. Billy picked it up, and crumpled it into a ball.

I glanced around the ridge. Someone could have seen. There were houses up there. Someone could have watched Grampa waving the flag. Billy hurried behind us, trying to hide the white cloth, hide the red sun. In the distance, planes whined and groaned.

Papa! The thought slammed into me like a bullet. He could be right under those planes!

Mama was on the porch holding Kimi, looking into the sky, with Kimi clinging to her neck.

"Japanese planes, Mama . . . We're being bombed! We've got to get rid of the flag. . . . Grampa took it out to the field and waved it. Someone might have *seen."*

Mama squinted up, raised a hand to her eyes. "That's just army planes . . . like always. . . ."

"No, Mama . . . They're bombing . . . down by Pearl Harbor! We saw from the trees."

Two planes banked overhead, the red suns striking down like hot stones. Mama stared at them. It suddenly all made sense to her. *"Bury* it," she said, her eyes wide with fear. "Bury that flag." She ran inside the house and brought back Grampa's photograph of the emperor. "Bury this too. . . . Go! Now!"

Grampa ran to get a shovel. Billy and I dove under the house and managed to dig a hole with our hands. Lucky's puppies surrounded us. Billy shoved them out of the way. They came back, and Billy put them in the pen.

When we came out from under the house, Grampa was standing in the yard with the shovel. He gave us a sorrowful look, then walked away, slowly, out to the jungle.

More planes circled overhead. They leveled out and sped away. The ships in the harbor had to be nothing but melting steel by now.

Down by the grocery store you could still see a blur of smoke from the explosion, an ugly smudge in the sky.

"I gotta get home," Billy said, squinting up at it. "Quick! Maybe Charlie's picking this up on his radio."

We started to run off, but Mama called to me. "Tomi, you find out, then you come home. . . ."

Kimi peeked up at the sky and started clawing at Mama's arms.

"Tomi!" Mama yelled. "Run!" She covered Kimi's head with her hand and ran back into the house. Another fighter thundered in from behind me and Billy, coming right at us.

Kimi was screaming inside the house.

I fell to the dirt and covered my head. So did Billy. Machine guns started spitting, the *bop-bop-bop-bop-bop* jabbing down. I cringed. Squeezed into a ball.

But the plane flew past.

I peeked up and saw it drop lower as it headed up the valley, shooting at something near the cemetery. Billy and I leaped up and ran after it, trying to catch a last glimpse. The fighter dropped even lower, then disappeared below the treetops, guns still wailing. Seconds later, it shot back up into the sky.

The air smelled like gunpowder. So much was happening, it made me dizzy. Little stars exploded in my eyes. I shook them away and took a deep breath. My arms started stinging, and I looked at them. Long, thin red lines of dried blood. I must have scratched them coming down the tree.

"Come on," Billy said. "Charlie's radio!"

I got up and ran toward the jungle, following Billy. Behind us, Kimi's terrified screams filled the air. I stumbled through the bushes, the trees. I kept running, but not thinking. All I asked was to stay on my feet, to follow Billy and be stronger than my rubbery bones. "Papa," I heard myself call. "Papa . . ."

11

Jackhammers

Billy's shirt floated ahead of me like a ghost. Planes kept droning on, out of sight above the trees. We were all going to *die!* They were going to bomb the whole island, bomb everything!

Thoomp, thoomp, thoomp . . .

"Billy!" I called. But he didn't stop running. Green and yellow colors shot through the spaces in the trees, coming down like diamonds from the sun, everything spinning, spinning, spinning. . . .

"Tomi," Charlie said, his hand suddenly on my shoulder. "Tomi, you okay?" He shook me. Billy was there too. He stared at me with his mouth slightly open.

"Tomi." Charlie squeezed my shoulder.

"I'm okay," I said. "I'm . . . I'm . . ."

"Come inside." Charlie pulled me into the house. My

legs were trembling. Billy put his hand on my back and followed me.

"This is no maneuver. . . ."

The voice on Charlie's radio was tinny. Lots of static.

"This is the real McCoy!"

Charlie leaned forward, sitting on the edge of a chair. He kept his fingers on the dial, like he was guarding it from drifting off the station. I noticed that the thumping explosions and rattle of antiaircraft fire had stopped. All I could hear was an occasional pop, like a firecracker.

"The United States Army Intelligence has ordered that all civilians stay off the streets. Do not use your telephone. Stay off the streets. Keep calm. Keep your radio turned on for further news. Get your car off the street. Fill water buckets and tubs with water, to be ready for a possible fire. Attach garden hoses . . ."

Another wave of excitement and fear ran through me, like when you're sick with a fever. I glanced over at Charlie's clock. Eight-forty. Only an hour ago I'd been catching pop flies with Billy.

Thoomp . . . thoomp.

The bombing started up again.

The planes came back, droning high overhead. Billy and I ran out into the yard. Charlie followed us, but more cautiously, peeking out the door first. Now the air smelled like burning rubber.

"Japanee plane," Charlie said, shaking a fist at the sky. "Damn Japanee plane."

"We better get some hoses up to the house," Billy said.

Charlie nodded, and the three of us hurried over to the toolshed. Together we dragged six heavy garden hoses up the driveway. Billy's brother was nowhere in sight.

The rumbling grew in the distance. More planes dotted the sky, like a swirl of flies, some circling out over the ocean, some heading toward the mountains and banking back toward Pearl Harbor. "We'd be better off hiding in the jungle," Billy said. "They're not going to bomb trees."

Ka-booom!

The earth rocked. A shudder rumbled through the dirt under my feet.

"There!" Billy said, pointing to a cloud of black smoke rolling skyward. It looked like it was over the ridge near our school. You couldn't tell for sure.

Another plane burst past and shot up the valley. A wide path of earth and trees shivered beneath it. It was so close you could see the rivets on the wings, and the red sun.

We got the hoses hooked up and ran back to Charlie's radio. The announcer said they needed doctors and nurses and shipyard workers and ROTC boys, even Boy Scouts.

"*. . . a warning to all people throughout the territory of Hawaii and especially on the island of Oahu. . . . In the event of an air raid, stay under cover. Many of the wounded have been hurt by falling shrapnel from antiaircraft guns. . . . If an air raid should begin, do not go out-of-doors. Stay under cover. . . . You may be seriously injured or instantly killed by shrapnel from falling antiaircraft shells.*"

"I gotta go," I said, suddenly remembering Mama and Kimi. I started out the door.

"Tomi," Charlie said. "You folks need anything, you come see me. . . . Okay?"

"Okay . . ."

I turned to Billy. So much had happened. "Watch yourself," he said, trying to smile.

"Yeah . . . you too."

• • •

The planes vanished again, sometime after nine-thirty, leaving behind mile-high stacks of black and gray smoke that spread out over the island like a dirty fishnet.

An hour passed.

No planes. No explosions.

I stood on the porch, watching the sky, and filled buckets of water that I put by the front and back doors. In case there was a bomb. In case there was a fire.

Another hour . . . into the afternoon . . . the island calming, calming. The muffled crackling of ack-ack still popped, but only every once in a while.

The waiting was worse than anything. What would come next? Would they come back? Would they start bombing houses? Would they land on the beaches? And Papa . . . where was he? Did he even know what had happened?

For the first time I could ever remember, I saw Mama crying. She stayed in the kitchen, cutting green onions and seaweed for miso soup, and washing dishes, then drying them on a towel—did all kinds of normal things—but all the time crying silently. Tears rolled down her cheeks

in thin wet lines. I hated seeing that. *It's okay, Mama,* I
wanted to say. The planes were gone.

But it wasn't okay.

Mama noticed me watching her and wiped her cheeks
with the back of her hand. "Go find Kimi," she said in a
calm voice. "She hiding somewhere. . . . See if she all
right, Tomi."

And where was Grampa?

I found Kimi in Mama's closet. I tried to get her to
come out, but she wouldn't. Wouldn't even say a word.

"Come on, Kimi," I pleaded. "It's quiet now. . . .
It's all over."

She shook her head.

I squatted down and opened the door a little farther.
"Pretty dark in here, isn't it?"

She nodded, clutching her old Raggedy Ann doll.

"Come," I said. "Let's go outside. It's okay now. . . .
I'll show you."

She shook her head again.

"How about if I get Azuki Bean from under the house
for you?"

Kimi nodded.

"Yeah. Good. Let's go get her."

She pushed at me to get out of the way. When we got
to the front door, Kimi stiffened up, and wouldn't move.

"Okay, wait here," I said. "I'll go get Azuki Bean."

Lucky was lying with her puppies, trembling. I stroked
her head. "I know how you feel, girl." She licked the
back of my hand when I cupped it around Azuki Bean,
who was snuggled up against Lucky's warm belly. Azuki

Bean was small and fat and soft and sweet-smelling. "Okay, girl. I got a job for you."

Sitting just inside the screen door, Kimi snuggled Azuki Bean in her lap next to Raggedy Ann. Azuki Bean was a girl, Grampa had finally figured out. Red was a boy. Azuki Bean rubbed her wet nose against Kimi's hand, and Kimi smiled up at me.

"Good dog," I whispered.

A flock of birds raced by, their shadows streaking over the grass. The pigeons! "Kimi, look," I said, pointing to the birds. "I'll be right back, okay?"

Kimi nodded, and looked down at Azuki Bean.

Fourteen pigeons had returned. Three were still missing. I fed them and latched the door. If a pigeon didn't come back in three days, you'd have to wait a week or more before it returned. If it did.

• • •

Billy came over a couple of hours later. His father had called and said he'd be home as soon as he could get there, but it might be a while. They were okay, but the city was in a mess. Billy said his mother went straight to work at the hospital right after the bombing started. His father was at the harbor.

"Those fires are still burning down by the school," Billy said, pointing from the porch. "You can see the smoke."

Just then Grampa came walking around the house from the back, carrying a bucket of eggs. Eggs? Spooky . . . eggs at a time like that.

"Good, nah?" Grampa said, looking over at me and Billy. He smiled and held up the bucket.

"What?" I asked. "The *eggs?*"

Grampa nodded, a quick dip of his head. *"Tamago."* He put the bucket down, and one by one took the eggs out and arranged them in a neat line on the top step.

"Grampa . . . ?"

"For soldiers."

"What soldiers?"

"From plane."

I frowned at him. "What are you *talking* about?"

"Soldiers come, I give egg . . ."

"I think he means Japanese soldiers," Billy said.

I stared at Grampa. Was he *joking?* Had he lost his mind? Oh, Papa, where are you? Come home. . . . Come home *now.*

"Where that flag?" Grampa asked.

Before I could say anything, I heard the tramping sound of boots pounding on dry dirt. Billy's mouth dropped open. I turned around. Eight U.S. Army guys charged toward us with rifles and bayonets pointing at our stomachs. They spread out around the front of the house, dust settling at their feet, sweat pouring down from under their helmets.

"You live here?" one of the men asked Grampa.

Grampa looked a little surprised. I think he really was expecting Japanese soldiers. But he caught himself and bowed. "Good afternoon, officers," he said in his best English, then pointed toward the eggs.

"Yes," I said, quickly stepping in front of him. "We live here."

"We got a report that someone around this area was signaling the Jap fighters. . . . You know anything about that?"

"N-no," I said.

He looked at Billy, and Billy shook his head.

"Think hard, boys. This is *extremely* serious. This is war. . . . Tell me anything you might have seen. We were told the Japs dropped parachuters up the valley, and that someone around here was signaling them with a flag."

"We didn't see any parachuters," I said.

If I told him about Grampa's flag they'd shoot him. Shoot *us*.

The man turned to Billy. "Who are you?"

"Billy Davis, sir. I live next door."

"You see anything?"

Billy stared at the man. He didn't answer.

Mama opened the door, then stepped back inside. The door hinges squeaked as the door sprang back.

"Come on out here, ma'am," the man said, then turned back to Billy.

"Did you *see* anything?" he asked again.

"No, sir."

"Think! This is very, very serious."

"I didn't see anyone signaling any parachuters."

The man studied Billy's face. He turned to Grampa. Glared at him, glared at Mama. Then, with a quick wave of his hand, he left. The men jogged off behind him, heading through the trees toward diamond grass.

We watched them go. Silence spread, huge and strange, like the silence in the eye of a hurricane. Little riffles of thought tried to organize something in my brain.

Grampa sat down on the steps next to his eggs and stared off into the trees. I couldn't tell if he was scared or dazed or what.

"I . . . better get going," Billy finally said. He turned and walked away, looking back once.

Thanks . . . for not telling, I wanted to say.

Billy hurried into the trees. I stared until the last hint of him had vanished.

Grampa sat with his elbows on his knees and his head in his hands, staring at the ground. I sat down next to him and watched a trail of ants go in and out of a crack in the dry earth.

• • •

Just before dark, Charlie came over and told us that the territory had been placed under martial law. Major General Walter C. Short was now the governor of the islands. "And you gotta make the windows black," Charlie said.

Mama invited him in, but he said he had to get back up to the Davises' house and help Billy and Jake. "The parents not home yet. . . . No forget the blackout. . . . No can have any kind light show through from inside the house."

Mama thanked him and gave him six of Grampa's eggs.

"Lucky got water tank your house," Charlie told me

after Mama had gone back inside. "The radio said they went poison the water supply in the mountains."

"Really?"

"That's what they said."

Charlie left. Mama hung blankets up over the back door and the windows in the kitchen. I found a candle and lit it. Kimi, Grampa, Mama, and I ate a small meal of pickled vegetables and rice, then sat in the hot, airless room, dripping with sweat until we couldn't take it anymore.

Finally, Mama blew out the candle. We moved into the dark front room and tried to sleep, huddled together on the floor. I got one of Papa's fishing knives and kept it next to me, in case we were attacked in the middle of the night. Through the screen door, you could see a reddish glow above the trees from the fires that still burned at Pearl Harbor.

I couldn't sleep.

Could anyone? With the whole island blacked out, it was the blackest of black nights. I nearly stopped breathing when I heard a papery, rustling sound somewhere under the house. Rats, or Lucky . . . maybe a mongoose. I slid down under my blanket and curled up into a ball.

A little later, the whole island came alive with machine-gun fire and explosions. Somewhere down in the city, or maybe it was in the mountains. Searchlights exploded across the black sky, slicing the clouds like glowing white bayonets. I peeked up and watched from where I lay, the lights framed by the screen door. The whole thing lasted only a few minutes.

Then the lights went out.

The guns stopped.

Kimi cried softly in Mama's arms. Grampa and I got up and crept out to the porch. I looked around the yard, but couldn't see anything that shouldn't have been there. Were Japanese soldiers landing on the beaches? Were they in the hills and working their way down? Were they in reloaded planes heading back, just minutes offshore?

After a while, Grampa and I went inside and lay down on the floor again. Mama didn't ask us what we'd seen out there. I finally dozed off, but woke sometime later to a muffled, rattling sound . . . nearby . . . but not too close . . . a rattling, like guns . . . no, not guns . . . something else.

Grampa was gone.

I got up and felt my way out to the front porch, the old floorboards creaking under me. Outside, the trees surrounded the yard in huge black blobs that swayed in the breeze, leaves hissing. The air was cool. A gunpowdery smell mixed with burning rubber.

The rattling sounded louder on the porch.

Jackhammers . . . that's what it sounded like . . . jackhammers. But in the middle of the night?

"They digging graves," someone said.

I jumped back.

Grampa stood below me, hidden in the dark blur of the yard.

"Criminy, Grampa!"

He climbed the steps halfway, then sat down slowly, as if he'd just discovered how old he really was. I went down and sat next to him.

"Who's digging graves?"

"Army mens . . . up the cemetery . . . bodies from Paru Haba."

Bodies? It hadn't even occurred to me that people had been *killed* down there.

"Lot of bodies, Tomikazu . . . lot of bodies."

"Did you go up there and look?"

"Lot of dead peoples."

Grampa and I sat in the dark without speaking, listening to the jackhammers. After a while we went back inside. Grampa lay down on his mat. He crossed his arms over his chest and stared at the ceiling.

I woke several times again. Jackhammers. Noises in the yard. Grampa's rooster, off schedule. The black dead of night made every little fear bigger. I almost couldn't stand it. Every movement in the trees outside was a Japanese soldier sneaking up to the house. . . . Every *dut-dut-dut-dut-dut* of the jackhammers at the cemetery brought back the faces of dead people staring out from the magazines at Billy's house. . . . Every distant barking dog was a warning that when the sun finally rose we would be looking down the barrels of enemy guns.

Dut-dut-dut-dut-dut.

I covered my ears.

Dut-dut-dut-dut-dut.

Dut-dut-dut-dut-dut.

12

Messenger Birds

Bam! Bam! Bam! Bam! Bam! "Open up in there!" *Bam! Bam! Bam!*

The screen door rattled like it would fall off. I bolted up with a pounding heart, staring at the dark shadow of a man in the doorframe.

"Whatchoo want?" I heard Grampa say. He was coming out of the kitchen, Mama following him.

"Taro Nakaji . . . Does he live here?"

Six-thirty. Dark, wet morning. I staggered up as Grampa opened the door. "Please . . . come inside," Mama said, bowing in the Japanese way.

"Taro Nakaji," the man said without coming into the house. He was tall. A khaki uniform showed under his rainslicker. Army. A pistol was strapped to his belt. Two policemen in olive-brown uniforms, also wearing slickers, stood behind him on the porch. One of them was looking around the yard. A Hawaiian guy. Gray clouds moved in the sky beyond, the wind pushing them toward the sea.

"He fishing," Mama said.

"Fishing?"

"Three days ago, he went. Come home tomorrow, or next day after that."

The army man glanced around the front room. "You have a radio?"

Mama shook her head.

Kimi sneaked up and peeked around Mama's legs.

"You mind if we look around?" the man asked.

"Please," Mama said. "Look the house . . . please . . ."

Grampa stepped back and let them pass. He studied them closely. We waited in the front room while the three men searched the house in less than a minute. When they finished, the army guy went over to Grampa and said, "Someone reported that you kept messenger pigeons. . . . How long have you been sending messages to the enemy?"

Mama made a small gasping sound, then covered her mouth with her hand. Grampa scowled at the man.

"They're not messenger birds," I said. "They're racing pigeons, and some other kinds."

"Shhh, Tomi," Mama said. "No talk like that to this man."

The army man glared at me, like he was trying to keep what I looked like in his mind. I thought he was going to slug me. I looked at the floor.

The local guy came over and put his hand on my shoulder. "Listen, son. We're just doing what we have to do. If there are enemy agents around here, we have to find them. . . . Do you understand that?"

"Yes . . . I do."

"Good. So can you show us the pigeons?"

I nodded, still looking at the floor.

Grampa and I led them out into the yard. A fine light rain was falling. Lucky barked at the men and Grampa shushed her. Mama and Kimi watched from the porch.

The army man stopped at the wire clothesline and nodded to one of the policemen. Mama watched him cut the wire and loop it around his hand.

What was going *on?*

"Let's go," the army man said, waiting for me and Grampa.

We headed into the trees. The cold, muddy path pressed up between my toes. The air smelled clean again. No gunpowder. And the jackhammers from last night had stopped. When we got to the edge of the field, I pointed with my chin to the lofts. The army man glanced around the field, then strode over to the pigeons with the rest of us following silently.

He studied the birds, his face blank. His eyes never even blinked. Spooky. A sudden gust of wind and rain rushed into the field. Little rivers ran down the guy's slicker. Me and Grampa were getting soaked.

"Destroy them," the man said to Grampa.

It took a couple of seconds to hit me.

"What!" I said.

The local guy grabbed my arm. "Hold on, son. They have to go."

"But *why?* They're just racers. . . . No one sends any

messages on them." The policeman's grip was rock tight, now holding both of my arms.

"I'm sorry," the army man said. "We're at war."

Silence.

"Go on," he ordered Grampa. "Kill them."

The policeman let me go and I ran over to Grampa. "No, *ojii-chan* . . . no . . ." Grampa put his hand on my neck. He pulled me close to him. He'd never done that before. In that moment I knew the birds would die.

"Grampa . . . ?"

"Go back house," he said. "Get knife. . . . Get two . . . sharp ones. *Go!*" He shoved me away.

I ran back through the trees. *Destroy . . . Kill . . .* Why? What did the pigeons have to do with anything?

I leaped up the steps to the porch and burst into the front room. "Mama! Mama!"

She was in the kitchen with Kimi, cutting an apple.

"I need . . . I need two sharp knives." I tried to slow down, remembering too late not to scare Kimi. I took deep breaths, gulped, and swallowed air.

"Fish knife," Mama said softly. Did she *know* this would happen?

Kimi's dark eyes were as round as plums.

I took Papa's two fish-cleaning knives, then ran back outside. The screen door slapped against the house. *Kill* the birds. Why? Who even knew how to put any kind of message on them? And where would they fly to? Japan? Stupid!

The two policemen watched me run toward them, their arms crossed, frowning from under their plastic-covered flat-topped hats. Grampa stood next to them, looking small, but strong in his stubborn way. My eyes pleaded with him to say something, to tell me they'd changed their minds.

I slowed down and walked up to the army man. I offered him the two knives, handles forward, the oiled blades razor-sharp and dark with age.

"Not me, son. You and the old man."

"*Me?*" I said.

Grampa reached over and took one of the knives. He ran his thumb over the cutting edge, then, without looking at me, pointed the knife to the loft the racers were in. "You get those," he said. "I get these ones."

I turned to the policeman, the nice one. He shook his head.

Without a word, Grampa and I reached in and removed the pigeons one by one and silently bled them to death with quick, clean slits across the throat. Blood spurt out over my arms, my shirt, dripped from my hands, landed on my feet. We dropped the fluttering bodies to the grass, one by one. When we were done, we laid them all in a long line on the ground. The blood turned the wet grass a glistening red-brown. A sourness rose from my stomach, swelled at the back of my throat, like gasoline. I could barely see through my flooding eyes.

The memory of the gentle cooing of thirty-five silky-feathered pigeons slowly died away, faded away, bled away . . . and, finally, in silence, flowed down into the earth forever.

I stood looking down at the silent line of bodies. They never had a chance. They just had to take it.

Grampa reached over and took my knife, then put

both knives on top of one of the lofts. He wiped his hands on his pants and faced the army man. "We are *'merican,"* he said, glaring into the man's eyes. "We talk Ing-lish. . . . We no make trouble."

I looked at Grampa like it was for the first time in my life. Grampa? Did *you* say that? You who gets your flag out and says *We are Japanese?*

His words . . . exactly like Papa's. Had they been in him all along? I suddenly felt so proud of that old man.

The army man nodded, then stared down at the bloody grass. After a moment he looked up. "I'm sorry, son . . ."

He paused, then said, "When your father gets home we will want to talk to him. But then, we'll probably catch him at the harbor."

The men left, bending a trail of wet grass toward the trees. Why Papa? What did he do?

"Kuso," Grampa whispered, kneeling down by the birds. His hands were red, sticky with blood. I rubbed mine on my bloody shirt. I rubbed and rubbed, but the blood stuck to me. I ripped the shirt off and threw it into the bushes. I never wanted to see it again.

Grampa put his hand on my shoulder. "Come, boy. We take home, put on ice . . . at least can eat, nah?"

Careful to keep the pigeons out of Kimi's sight, Grampa and I plucked and washed the birds out behind the water tank. We wrapped them in old rice bags and hid them in the back of Mama's ice box until Mama and Grampa could spread them among their friends.

After that, Grampa and I washed our hands, side by

side. Then Grampa went out to his chickens, to be alone. But I stayed at the water tank and washed and washed and washed and washed.

I crawled under the house and sat cross-legged in the dirt with Lucky's puppies tumbling in and out of my lap, nudging each other and taking turns gnawing on my fingers. I felt hollow and sick. I wanted to throw up. But I couldn't.

• • •

It was Monday, and Mama should have been up at the Wilsons' house, working. She was so confused she didn't know what to do. She was scared to death to go there after what had happened. She finally decided to go anyway, but when she got there Mrs. Wilson wouldn't let her in the house. Mama's eyes were red and puffy when she came back home.

Later that afternoon Mama decided to go to the grocery store. And she wanted me to go with her, to help carry things. It took all my effort to drag myself along behind her.

There was a long line outside the store. A man was trying to close the door. "We're running out of food," he said, which only caused everyone to push forward. He gave up and left the door open.

While we were waiting, I found that morning's newspaper on the ground. I read the headline to Mama. "RAIDERS RETURN IN DAWN ATTACK."

Mama stared ahead with a stony look on her face. I'd

heard gunfire during the night, but I hadn't heard anything in the morning. When did they return? And where?

I read more.

Renewed Japanese bombing attacks on Oahu were reported as Honolulu woke to the sound of antiaircraft fire in a cold, drizzling dawn today. Citizens were warned to be on watch for parachutists reported in Kalihi.

Red antiaircraft bursts shot into the cloudy skies from the direction of Hickham Field, which was reported bombed again at about 6 A.M.

Warning that a party of saboteurs had been landed on northern Oahu was given early Sunday afternoon by the army. The saboteurs were distinguished by red disks on their shoulders.

I went on reading silently, caught up in the story. It was *Honolulu* I was reading about, not someplace on the other side of the world.

"Read," Mama said.

Certain enemy agents have been apprehended and detained, General Short announced.

He warned all citizens to "watch their actions carefully." Any infractions of military rules will be "swiftly and harshly dealt with."

I cringed as I remembered Grampa running out into the field with his flag. He could *still* be shot for doing that. I folded the paper to show to Papa when he came home.

Mama and I waited in silence. Everyone around us

was quiet too. But farther ahead I could hear people talking, and farther behind us. It felt strange, like people were sneaking glances at us.

I studied the dirty paint on the side of the store. Soon a gap appeared between Mama and me and the people behind us. In front of us there was also a gap. I looked behind me again, this time into the eyes of a lady glaring straight into mine. In my whole life, I'll never forget that look. I realized that what that lady saw wasn't just a boy and his mother. . . . What she saw was a *Japanese* boy, and his *Japanese* mother.

• • •

Later that day, after we'd managed to buy only one small bag of rice and six onions, Mama told me to hang the blackout blanket back up over the kitchen window. I poked one corner onto a nail and was about to hang the other when I saw something outside, a movement in the trees and bushes at the edge of the yard. I kept a small triangle of blanket open, peeking out. A hand parted some low branches. I saw part of a face. The bushes jiggled, and the shadowy figure slunk away, back into the trees. Dog tags. Tinkling.

13

Rumors

I tossed around in my bed trying to sleep, but kept waking from dreams of blood . . . pumping from pigeons' throats. Once I gasped and sat up, feeling the warm blood streaking down my arms from my hands, dripping off my elbows.

Grampa was a motionless lump on the floor. No sounds came from his mat, not even the usual whistle of his breathing.

"Ojii-chan," I whispered. "You awake?"

He didn't answer, and I was afraid he'd died in his sleep. I got out of bed and looked closely at him. Still no sounds, no movement. I bent down and touched him.

"We have been *disgraced,"* he said in Japanese, making me jump back. I couldn't tell if he was awake or if he was dreaming. He fell silent again, and I went back to bed.

• • •

The next morning—Tuesday—I went over to Billy's with my schoolbooks. It felt crazy to do that. But I didn't know what else to do.

No one answered when I knocked on the door. Billy's house was as quiet as a church. I found Charlie squatting in the Davises' garden, pulling weeds, as if nothing had changed.

"Where's Billy?"

"Gone . . . They all gone . . . went to help out somewheres."

"What about school?"

Charlie shook his head. "No more . . . Canceled."

He stood up and brushed the dirt from his hands, then came over and put his arm around my shoulder. "Come, Tomi. . . . We go down your place. . . . I need to talk to Grampa . . . and Mama." Charlie was silent the whole way over, thinking about something.

"Mama," I called when we got there. "Charlie's here."

Mama came out of the kitchen wiping her hands on a towel. She greeted Charlie with a bow. "Come inside, Charlie-san."

He slipped off his boots and stepped in. "How you, Mama-san?" Charlie asked. "You need anything?"

"We okay," Mama said. "Thank you."

The screen door out in the kitchen slapped shut, and Grampa came into the front room with two cans of eggs. "Twenty-three," he said, lifting the cans.

Charlie smiled, but only for a moment. "You folks heard? The U.S. went declare war on Japan."

Mama looked surprised, then sad. She looked down at the floor. Grampa put the eggs on the couch, and folded his arms. I hadn't seen a newspaper since the one I'd found at the store.

"That's not all," Charlie added. "The army and the FBI arresting plenty Japanee men, and some Italian and German, but mostly Japanee." Charlie shook his head. "They say they help plan for attack Pearl Harbor. . . . They say the fishermens been taking fuel out to submarines. . . ."

"Fishermen?" I said.

Charlie nodded. "They going arrest your daddy, Tomi. . . . They going arrest all the fishermens. And they going arrest language school teachers, Japanee businessmens, Buddhist priests, like that."

Mama sat down on the couch. She took a deep breath and closed her eyes, then opened them.

"More better you folks stay close to home for a couple of days," Charlie said. "Everybody nervous about Japanee, and lots of people with guns and machete out there. They looking for revenge. And rumors going 'round now. Most of them crazy kind things, but you never know, I guess. . . . That's what people saying about Japanee. . . . They say: you never know about them."

"You never know what?" I asked.

"They saying you never know about how maybe was true they went help show the planes where to bomb. There was one story about somebody went cut big arrows in the sugarcane fields that pointed to Pearl Harbor. And there was one about how they went check the Japanee pilots who was shot down and found McKinley High School rings on the finger . . . and they saying the water supply was poisoned . . . and that local Japanee peoples are hiding ammunition on their properties.''

That was so crazy.

Charlie frowned at the floor. He rubbed his hand over his mouth, then looked up at Grampa. "Taro-san got a radio on that boat? Or a U.S. flag?''

Grampa shook his head.

Charlie ran his fingers through his hair. Twice, like he was thinking hard. He looked at me . . . then Mama. "The paper said today, they going shoot any boat come toward the island if no got one U.S. flag on top.''

Silence.

Grampa turned away and looked out the screen door.

"Sorry," Charlie said. "You folks need anything, you come get me. Don't go *anywheres*. Very dangerous.''

Charlie slipped his boots back on. "Tomi . . . you gotta be the one to go outside for what you need. They going give Joji-san hard time because he's old timer, yeah? But you just a kid. And you, Mama-san . . . no talk Japanee, no bow like one Japanee, and no wear any kind Japanee clothes, kimono, like that. . . . And got one curfew now, sundown to sunrise . . . nobody go out after dark . . . bombye they going shoot you.''

Charlie glanced around at all of us, then left. Grampa went over to the door and watched him walk back through the trees. Mama stayed on the couch, keeping to herself.

Finally, she said in a soft but firm voice, "We going through this house to find everything that could bring trouble . . . photograph, letter . . . everything. . . . We going bury 'um."

*   *   *

By noon, everything we had that had anything to do with Japan was spread out over the kitchen table—Mama's beautiful traditional kimono; a bundle of letters tied together with white ribbon; a photograph of me when I was younger, standing in the front row of my language school class with a Japanese flag in the background; Grandma's altar; incense wrapped in thin paper; the family *katana,* and a few other things that Mama and Grampa had found.

We all stood around the table, silently touching this and that, picking things up and looking them over, then putting them down again.

"Bury it," Mama finally said, her eyes glistening.

I reached toward the *butsudan* and Grampa stopped me with a touch on my arm. Gently, he picked up the altar himself, and taking only that and the *katana,* went outside to hide them in the jungle. My throat started to burn. I quickly wrapped what was left in a burlap bag, then took it under the house and buried it near Grampa's flag.

*   *   *

Moments after I came back out from under the house, I caught Keet Wilson sneaking around the yard again, only this time he saw me. And this time Jake was with him. I went over to the water tank and washed the dirt off my hands.

At first I ignored them, hoping they'd go away. I worried that they'd seen me come out from under the house. I kept scrubbing my already clean hands with my back to them.

"Hey, fish boy," Keet said. "How's your messenger birds?"

Messenger birds. He'd never called them that before.

I could see him out of the corner of my eye, a moving shape. He strolled over and stood next to me, fingering his dog tags.

Still I didn't look at him. I wiped my hands on my pants, and tried to scowl like Grampa.

Keet snickered and said, "Well, anyway, tell your mother not to bother coming to work at our house anymore. In fact, my father is considering kicking you off our property. . . . We don't want to support any Jap sympathizers."

Don't shame this family, Tomi. . . .

"You hear what I said?"

Shame yourself, and you shame us all. . . .

I bunched up my lips.

"*Hey!* I'm talking to you." Keet shoved me and I staggered backward.

"Keet!" Jake said, grabbing his shoulder. "Stop it. . . . He's just a kid. . . ."

Keet whirled around and swung at Jake, landing a

blow that glanced off the side of Jake's head. Jake bent over and grabbed his ear. You could see it hurt pretty bad. "You're gonna be sorry you did that," Jake said.

Keet charged into Jake. The two of them tumbled to the ground, grunting and spitting. Jake rolled away and scrambled to his feet. He stood over Keet, looking down with his fists clenched. "Get up and fight like a man."

Keet wiped his mouth with his knuckle, smearing some blood. He pushed himself up and brushed the dirt from his clothes. Then, without looking at Jake or me, he strode away. Jake watched with fists still clenched and ready.

"Sorry about your pigeons," Jake said, when Keet was out of sight. "And sorry about Keet. Sometimes he just gets crazy."

Jake started to leave, but turned back. "It was him, you know. . . . He told the police about your birds."

• • •

Just before the sun went down, Grampa rode off on his bicycle. He was halfway to the trees when I saw him.

"Grampa!" I yelled from the porch. "The curfew!"

But he just kept on going. I should have known that even Charlie's warning couldn't keep him from doing something if he wanted to. I watched him weave around the holes and bumps in the path, the rusted silver fenders rattling all the way down to the street.

I sat on the bottom step. Lucky came up to me. "Crazy old man," I muttered, and Lucky licked my cheek. She had a couple of new ticks in her coat, and I started picking them off.

Mama and Kimi came out on the porch and stood above me.

"Where's Grampa going?" I asked.

"Kewalo . . . see if the boat came back."

"But what about what Charlie said?"

"Ojii-chan is *ojii-chan."*

Still nervous about being outside, Kimi inched down to sit next to me.

"Ticks," I said.

She watched with great concern as I picked one off and smashed it on the step with a stone. Blood spurted out and she pinched up her face in fascinated disgust.

Lucky panted patiently. I squeezed another tick off and she tried to nip my hand.

"It's okay, girl. . . . I got it." I showed it to her and she sniffed at it.

Mama went back into the house. Kimi got up to follow her. "Wait," I said. "Stay out here awhile. . . . We can go see if the lost pigeons came home." She settled back down on the step and pressed her warm arm against mine.

The day was slipping away, shadows deepening. But I managed to get Kimi to head over to the trees with me. She practically squeezed my hand off.

Diamond grass was quiet. We walked out to the middle of the field and looked up at the purple sky.

"Isn't that color something, Kimi?"

I looked down at her and she nodded.

"Mr. Ramos says the sky goes up and up and never

ends." No matter how hard I tried, I still couldn't believe that it never ended . . . and yet, I couldn't believe that it *did* end. Either way, it was impossible.

"Come on," I said, pulling Kimi along.

No birds had returned. The lofts were silent. Kimi yanked on my hand, wanting to get back to the house. I had to carry her through the shadowy trees, her arms tight around my neck. The bombs and planes still had her as scared as a wildcat.

• • •

Grampa was gone all night.

When he finally showed up in the morning, he went and tended his chickens before coming into the house. Mama and I watched him from the kitchen. I almost didn't want to hear what he'd found out, and I didn't think Mama did either.

Grampa came back with his morning eggs and set them on the table. "The police take 'um to jail," he said.

Mama gasped.

He was alive. . . .

Grampa sat down with a quick glance at Mama. "No can see 'um. No can get close."

Grampa motioned for me to sit. He put his hands on the table and stared at them for a while. "Sanji," Grampa said, "dead. . . . The 'merican planes went shoot the boat because no flag. . . ."

What? No, no, no . . . not Sanji. For a moment I was too stunned to move. Then the burning crybaby throat came back, and a quivering in my ears.

"Ohhh," Mama cried. "His wife . . . his little girl . . ."

Nobody said anything for a minute. Just looked at the table, the floor, the window, listened to the clock. Grampa sat with his own feelings locked deep inside him like always.

Sanji . . . *dead!* Did Papa wave at the planes before he knew they were shooting? Did he see Sanji get hit? And watch him *die?*

A tear rolled down Mama's face. She turned away so no one would see.

"Papa," Grampa said. "He going be all right, but got one bullet in the leg."

"What!"

"They shot the leg," Grampa said, refusing to look at me or Mama.

"They went take the boat and drag 'um inside Ala Wai canal," Grampa added. "They chop the bottom . . . sink 'um."

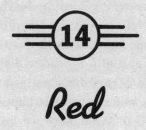

Red

A few days later, I took Kimi back out to the field. It was late afternoon, warm and still. School was still out, as far as I could tell. And I hadn't heard from Billy.

Like the rest of us, Kimi was used to having Papa gone for days at a time. But hardly ever more than a week. Now it had been more than *two* weeks since she'd seen him.

"Did Papa's boat sink?" she asked, looking up at me with her sad eyes. What could I say? What lie could I tell her?

"Papa's . . . gone somewhere for a while. . . . He'll be home soon."

Kimi turned away.

"Let's talk to him," I said.

"But how can he hear us?"

"I think he can hear every whisper that comes from

here," I said, tapping her heart. "All you have to do is close your eyes and think about what you want to say."

Kimi didn't answer for a while. Maybe she was trying to find just the right words. I knew how she felt. Ever since Grampa came home with the news about Papa I'd been lying awake at night. For hours I stared at the dark clouds that moved across the stars in my window. It was too hard to think about what was happening to Papa. I tried to be practical. What were we going to do? How would we live? We had Grampa's eggs, but that was practically nothing. We had the house, which the Wilsons let us use . . . but would they still let us stay there if they didn't want Mama to work for them? I had to get a job . . . but what about school? If we still had the boat I could . . . I could . . . What? An eighth-grader not even half Papa's size could do what? I shook the thoughts away.

Billy. Think of Billy. I hadn't seen him since the day he lied about Grampa and the flag. Where was he? Lots of *haoles* were selling their houses and running away to the mainland. It was spooky to see that. What if Billy's family went too? And what about the lie? How did that make Billy feel? I still shuddered just to think of it. Those soldiers would have shot Grampa, or even me and Billy, if they'd seen us with that flag.

"*Hato poppo,*" Kimi said.

"What?"

Kimi pulled on my arm. "*Hato poppo.*" She pointed toward the lofts.

At first I didn't see them in the shadows. But there they were, two of the three lost pigeons sitting on one of the lofts. "Hey, you're *right.*" For the first time in days, Kimi smiled.

We raced across the grass to the gentle, familiar sound of their cooing. "Blewww, blewww," I cooed back. "Where have you runaways been?"

I scooped some feed into a rusty coffee can, then rattled it. The pigeons stepped closer, walking sideways along the roof, heads bobbing and eyes on the coffee can. I emptied it into the feeder in the loft.

Whispering soft words like Papa had taught me, I reached up and cupped the pigeons in my hands and rubbed them against my cheek, one at a time. Then I let Kimi run a finger down their backs and put them into the loft. For a moment I wished the pigeons *were* messenger birds. . . . They could fly to Papa . . . take a note from Kimi . . . and Mama . . . then they'd come back. Come back . . .

Kimi smiled and clasped her hands together in front of her.

"Let's go tell Mama," I said, and Kimi grabbed my hand.

As we hurried back through the trees, I thought about Grampa. What would he say? Would he refuse to feed them so they'd go somewhere else? Or kill them?

"Mama," Kimi yelled, climbing the steps to the porch as fast as she could. "The *hato poppo* came home!" She disappeared into the house, the door slapping behind her. I waited outside at the bottom of the stairs for Grampa to come out. I knew he would.

After a few minutes the screen door creaked open, the rusty springs singing over the silence of the yard.

Grampa came out and closed the door gently. He stood at the top of the stairs, studying the darkening sky, his hands in the pockets of his wrinkled pants.

Finally, he glanced down at me and raised his chin toward the sunset sky. "Good, nah?" he said.

I nodded, and Grampa went back into the house.

• • •

A few days later, just before Christmas, I was out back with Grampa and the chickens, building more coops. Grampa was trying to increase the egg production so we'd have more to sell. Mrs. Wilson still hadn't asked Mama to come back to work. But Mr. Wilson hadn't kicked us off his land either.

We'd been working for about an hour when Grampa looked up from unrolling some wire. "The boy come look for you," he said.

"What boy?"

"Haole."

"Billy?"

Grampa nodded.

"When, Grampa? Why didn't you tell me sooner? What did he say?"

"Nothing . . . he only looking for you. That's all."

In Papa's toolshed I found some old fishing line and cut off about eight feet of it, then made a small loop on one end. I ran the other end through it and made a bigger loop.

Red, now about six weeks old, tripped along by my feet with the string leash keeping him from straying. At first he tried to bite it. All the way to Billy's house he jumped and stumbled and nipped at my feet.

I stopped at the edge of Billy's yard, and looked everything over before stepping out of the trees.

I knocked, but no one answered. I started around to the back of the house. Red was beginning to lag behind, so I picked him up.

Jake and Billy were down at the back edge of the yard. Jake was shoveling dirt into a burlap bag that Billy held open. Jake saw me first. Then Billy looked up.

I walked toward them with Red warm in the crook of my arm. Off to the right was a big, freshly dug hole. A long, sloping ramp with crude stairs chopped into the dark dirt ran down into it. Most of the hole was covered on top by pieces of lumber laid across it, like a roof.

"What's that?" I asked.

Billy wiped the sweat off his forehead with the back of his arm. "Bomb shelter."

"I haven't seen you in a while."

Billy looked down at his feet. "Yeah."

"What's that you got there?" Jake asked.

"Billy's dog."

"What?" Billy said, dropping the bag of dirt. I took the leash off and put Red on the grass. Billy came over and kneeled down. He stuck out his hand, and Red licked his dirty fingers. "Thanks . . ." Billy said, without looking up.

"I came by two times before," I said. "But no one was home."

"Yeah."

Jake leaned on the handle of the shovel. He looked at the ground when I glanced at him.

"Mom's been at the hospital a lot, and Dad joined the volunteers. Jake and I have been . . . busy . . . helping out," Billy said. He kept playing with Red without looking at me.

"Nothing personal," Jake said. "It hasn't been easy . . . know what I mean?"

"Dad told us to dig this hole," Billy said. "All we have to do now is put the dirtbags on the roof."

"Come on," Jake said to Billy. "We're almost done."

Billy stood up. "You want to help?"

I stared into his calm light blue eyes. Who was in them? Billy Davis of the Rats? Or someone different now?

"Sure," I said.

"Come on, then. Drag some of those bags over to the shelter and put them on the boards that go across the top."

Billy let Red roam while he and Jake went back to shoveling dirt. I dragged the loaded bags over to the wood roof. In about twenty minutes we were all standing there looking at it.

"Want to go down inside?" Jake asked.

"I guess so," I said.

"Watch those steps, though," Billy added. "Jake made them."

"Only because you couldn't, mudbrains."

Jake ducked under the lip of the roof and dropped down into the darkness. Billy went next, then me. Red came up and peeked down at us.

"The only thing that'll get you in here," Jake said, "is a direct hit."

"This is too creepy," Billy said.

Jake gave him a friendly shove. "You weeny." But he didn't waste any time following me and Billy back out into the sunlight.

Billy watched him walk back up to the house with the shovel, carrying it on his shoulder like a rifle. "Jake told Keet to take a hike after he found out Keet told the police about your birds. He feels really bad about that." Billy paused and kicked at the grass. "Dad's worried about Jake. He wants to quit school and join the army. . . . He's almost old enough."

At that moment I liked Jake as much as I liked Billy.

"Want to see something?" Billy asked.

"What?"

"Come."

Billy picked up Red and carried him into the jungle, following a thin path that zigzagged through the trees. I trailed behind, still thinking about Jake and Keet—and Mose and Rico. They seemed like men, almost. Now even Billy did, digging bomb shelters. Pretty soon we'd all be wearing camouflaged uniforms and steel helmets. But the papers said local Japanese who wanted to sign up couldn't, that they weren't loyal to the U.S. It was all wrong, like Papa in jail was wrong.

"They shot my father in the leg and arrested him," I told Billy.

"They *shot* him?"

"They sunk his boat, too . . . and . . . and they killed Sanji."

Billy stopped and looked back. "They *what?*"

"They weren't flying a flag. They never even knew they needed one. A plane shot up the boat."

"Aw, criminy," Billy said, squeezing his eyes shut and shaking his head. "Not Sanji . . . he was a good guy. . . . *Jeeze* . . . damn stupid war. Is your dad okay?"

"I think so."

We started walking again, Billy leading the way in silence. He kicked at the weeds in the trail, and though he tried to hide it, I saw him wipe his eyes with the back of his hand. I knew what he was feeling.

Soon sunlight fell through an opening in the trees.

"Over there," Billy said, his voice soft. He pointed to a big tree that was shattered and half burned. Everything around it was shredded.

"A bomb?"

"Dad thinks it was one of our own . . . a stray anti-aircraft shot."

We pushed through the shoulder-high ginger, Billy holding Red close to his chest. When we got to where the bomb landed, Billy kneeled down and pulled a piece of twisted shrapnel out of the dirt. "I can't believe Sanji's dead."

Silently we dug more pieces of metal out of the ground, and worked some out of the dead tree. Red rested in a spot of sunlight. For a moment I forgot about the war. It was me and Billy again . . . like it used to be. Only now we shared a sadness.

"You want to know why I didn't come see you for so long?" Billy said.

"Why?"

"Because of your grampa's flag. Because I lied about it." Billy sat in the dirt. "It's okay now, I guess. . . . I thought about it and decided that even if it happened again I'd still lie. . . . I know your grampa was only afraid, and not trying to signal or anything. . . ."

I picked up a clod of dirt and broke it up. What could I say?

Billy went on. "I hope your dad's okay."

"Me too."

We were quiet for a while. Then I said, "You want to go throw a ball around?"

"You still owe me fifteen cents, you punk."

"I can pay you in eggs."

"Forget it. I'll wait."

"So . . . what? You want to get your glove?"

Billy gave me his shy smile. "Yeah."

• • •

Billy got his glove and the ball that Mose and Rico had given him, and we started over toward my house with Red stumbling along behind.

"Hey, you got your ID card yet?" I asked. A teacher from Lincoln School had come to our house and signed me and Mama and Grampa up. She took our fingerprints and gave us cards that she said we had to carry everywhere we went. Since Kimi was only five, she didn't need one.

"Yeah," Billy said. "Kind of spooky, isn't it?"

"Spooky?"

"The cards . . . don't you know what they're for?"

"To identify who you are?"

"Yeah, but the main reason is to identify your body if there's another attack and you get killed."

• • •

When we got to diamond grass, Red was ready for a nap. Billy took him over and put him in the shade under one of the lofts.

I ran home and got my mitt. When I saw the fading ink of Keet's name written on it, I punched the glove that used to be his.

"I heard you had to kill the birds yourself," Billy said when I got back.

"Me and Grampa . . . we cut their throats."

Billy nodded toward the two birds in the loft. "What about those two?"

"They were out at the time. They were lucky."

"Can you keep them?"

"I don't know. But who's going to ask?"

"Right."

"Come on," I said. I didn't want to talk about the birds. I just wanted to get back to how it used to be. "Let's see if you can still throw a curveball."

"Shhh . . . are you kidding? I could make it circle your head and come back to me, if I wanted to."

"Yeah, yeah, yeah."

Thwack! The ball hit my mitt like a cannon shot. Still squatting, I tossed it back. Watching Billy catch it, just like it used to be, almost choked me up.

"Hey," Billy said, winding up.

"What?"

Thwack!

"Your grampa really *wasn't* cheering those planes on, was he? I mean with his flag?"

I stood, and studied the ball. "He hates them," I said. "They disgraced him. They disgraced a lot of people by doing what they did." I threw the ball back, hard.

Billy caught it and shook his hand out of his glove, and rubbed it. "Jeese, keep your hat on, already."

"Sorry."

"Yeah, me too."

I squatted down and waited for another pitch.

Billy bent forward, the ball in his hand behind his back.

"Thanks for telling me how you felt about the flag," I said.

"What flag? Quit talking, confonnit, and give me a sign."

I flashed two fingers. Billy nodded and whipped me a perfect curve.

Whock!

He smirked. "Want to see the one that goes around your head?"

15

Shikata Ga Nai

In the next days a voice started to nag at me, whispering words inside my mind. "Go now," it kept saying. "Go find Papa before it's too late. Go to the police." I couldn't stop thinking about it.

One morning, without saying anything to worry Mama, I went behind the house and got Grampa's bicycle out. I was just about to hop on it when Mose and Rico came walking up the trail from the street.

"Hey," Rico said with a big smile. Seeing them like that, so unexpectedly, made my throat burn, like when you're so sad about something you can't even cry. I felt like I hadn't seen Mose and Rico in over a year.

"How'zit," I managed to say, the burning stone stuck in my throat.

Mose and Rico both punched my arm, one after the other. "How you doing, cock-a-roach?" Rico said.

"Okay . . . How about you guys?"

"Still alive."

"Yeah, still alive," Mose added.

"Can you believe the Japanese went bomb us?" Rico said.

I shook my head and averted my eyes. I felt disgraced. Like Grampa.

Mose looked at me and asked, hesitantly, "They treating you okay, Tomi? . . . They come arrest your father . . . and your grandfather?"

"Not Grampa, just my father . . . They shot him in the leg and sunk his boat. And—and they killed his friend, Sanji . . . the planes did, U.S. planes. They shot at them on the boat. . . ."

"Aw, shee . . . that's bad," Mose said. "That's real bad."

We were quiet a moment, then Rico said, "Why they did that?"

"They weren't flying a U.S. flag."

"That's all?" Rico shook his head.

"Down by us," Mose said, "they got all the old Japanee guys and took 'um to Immigration. . . . They figure they naturally for Japan . . . but what they worried about? Those old guys no can do nothing."

"So what you folks going do?" Rico asked.

"I don't know. Grampa said to wait. But I can't. . . . I was just going down to the police station to see if I could find my father."

For a moment we stood there with nothing to say.

"You guys want to come?" I asked.

"Yeah, yeah," Rico said. "Sure, man. We got one cousin who works there."

"True," Mose added. "Some kind of desk job, though. Not a police."

There was another silent moment. Then I said, "You should see the looks we get from the people now. They think we're spies or something."

Rico shook his head. "That's crazy, man."

But Mose told the truth. "Still, nobody knows nothing ... so they scared ... just like we all scared."

Mose and Rico didn't have bikes, so the three of us started walking down to the police station, which was about three or four miles away. The streets were just like before the bombs—pretty clean, and people still walking around. Lots of people walking. Who had gasoline anymore? The army took it all and rationed a little bit to everyone else. Charlie said Mr. Davis could only get ten gallons a month. How we were going to get kerosene for our lamp and our stove was going to be a real problem soon.

Not everything on the streets was like before. In some places we passed streetlights shot out by blackout wardens, and burned or busted-up buildings that had been bombed, or hit by antiaircraft fire. At those places we stopped to look around before going on.

I was shocked. I hadn't seen anything but the grocery store since the day the planes came. But if it shocked Mose and Rico they were keeping it hidden.

"You heard about how they going give everyone a gas mask?" Rico said.

"Gas mask?"

"Yeah, they going give 'um to everyone. . . . Look stupit, those things."

"I guess they think they going come back and drop gas bombs," Mose added. "If I hear planes coming again, I going run for my place . . . *then* I put 'um on, but not before that."

"Hey," Rico said, "you heard about that car was driving to work up by your place? One plane came down with machine guns blasting and killed the guys inside?"

"Where by my place?"

"Judd Street, I think."

I remembered the plane that had scared Kimi . . . when Billy was there and we hit the dirt. Was that the plane Rico was talking about? If it was . . . spooky, boy.

"You know the day after the planes bombed Pearl Harbor?" I said. "That day, an army guy and two police came up to our house. They took our clothesline wire, and they made me and Grampa kill all my father's pigeons."

The two of them stopped and stared at me.

"Every one of them. It made me feel sick."

"But how come the pigeons?"

Because of Keet Wilson, I wanted to say. "Somebody told them we were sending messages on them."

"Messages?" Rico said, his eyes narrow. "Who were you sending the messages to?"

"Shuddup," Mose said, shoving Rico. "This is not a joke."

Rico looked confused. I didn't think he meant it as a joke.

"How come the army think like that?" Mose went on.

"They think you going send one message that says 'Those ships are here, by my house, come bomb us'? Stupit, man . . ."

"Just like the army, yeah?" Rico said.

"My grampa, he likes Japan . . . that's his homeland . . . but he didn't like what they did," I said. "We buried all our Japan things right after the army guy left. . . ." I paused, thinking of poor Grampa—so lost. "He's kind of confused now," I added, almost in a whisper.

"Lot of people confused," Mose said.

We started walking again. Rico said, "My father says the stupit army would be even more stupit if they didn't arrest all those old guys who still believe in Japan. Nobody knows if there was somebody who helped those planes, or what."

We walked awhile in silence. I had to admit that what Rico said made sense. How could anyone tell for sure? Maybe somebody really *did* send them a message, or even did something worse.

We passed a park where four men with no shirts on were digging a long trench for people to jump into if the bombing started up again. Two men swung picks and two shoveled dirt into pyramids along the edge. It reminded me of fresh graves up at the cemetery.

Rico finally broke the silence, the clinking sound of the picks fading away behind us. "My father said if the Japanee come back now, they going take us. They already knocked out almost all the navy ships and half the planes."

"It's gonna be bad, all right," Mose added. "What can we do now? Throw rocks?"

"That's right," Rico said. "I ain't letting those Japs take me, man." Rico looked at me, kind of embarrassed. "Sorry . . . everybody saying *Japs* now."

I looked down. "That's okay."

We walked another block. The clinking sound was gone.

"Anyway," I finally said. "If those Japs come back, they going to have to face us three ugly Rats, even if we only have stones."

Rico put his arm over my shoulder, and we walked the rest of the way bragging to each other about how we were going to bust their brains and tie them up and march them over to the stupit army and become heroes.

•   •   •

"We're too busy to fool around with you boys," the policeman said when we got to the police station. "Go on, now . . . get out of here."

"But I just want to know where he is, that's all . . . then we'll go. . . . Just tell me where he is."

The policeman frowned at me, but you could tell he was okay.

"How do I know where he is? The FBI took those men, not us."

"But *where* did they take them?"

"Shee," he said. "You pretty pushy. . . . I don't *know* where. . . . Sand Island is one place, but they have others too."

"Can you ask someone?"

"Listen . . ." He took a deep breath and shook his

head. "Okay, okay. I'll see what I can find out. . . . What's his name?"

"Nakaji, Taro."

"Wait here."

Me and Mose and Rico leaned against the wall by the door, trying to stay out of the way. I never saw so many police in one place in my whole life.

Another policeman came up to us. His shiny badge stood out like a fastball coming at your head. "How you boys doing?" he asked. "Somebody arrest you?"

Rico straightened up and shook his head.

The policeman laughed. "You boys should be out digging bomb shelters. They need volunteers everywhere."

"We going there next," Rico said, looking nervous.

"Good," the man said. "But be careful, yeah?"

"We will," Mose said, nodding his head vigorously.

The first policeman came back. "My best guess is Sand Island . . . but even if that's where he is, you can't see him, so don't waste your time. When they're ready to let you know something, they will."

I nodded. "Thanks, officer."

"That's okay. . . . Hey, it's tough on all of us right now." He studied us a moment, then said, "Go on, get out of here."

•   •   •

Later that day, after Mose and Rico had gone home, Mama wanted me to go looking for Grampa. She hadn't seen him all afternoon. I whistled for Lucky to come with me and she came trotting out from under the house with her tail wagging. That dog—she always made me feel good. Her puppies followed a little ways, then stopped and sat down. Lucky glanced back at them.

"Come on, girl," I said, snapping my fingers. "Let's go find Grampa."

The first place we went to was the chicken coop, where Grampa's prize Rhode Island Reds pecked around in the dirt and dozed in their beds of yellow straw. No Grampa.

Lucky and I followed the small trail that led into the jungle beyond the chickens. The weeds were so high they came up over my shoulders. Lucky walked ahead, sometimes disappearing, then coming back a little later.

Pretty soon we came to the stream. The water was cold and clear. I cooled my feet and Lucky lapped some of it up.

On the other side of the water was a dark and damp bamboo forest, loaded with mosquitoes. I had to keep slapping myself all over.

We came to a patch of tall grass that someone had recently walked through. Lucky sniffed ahead, following the new trail, getting pretty excited.

Soon we were in shade so deep I could hardly see the sky. I stopped to listen: the stream; a couple of birds chirping. That's all.

"Lucky," I whispered, but she was gone.

I crept to the edge of a small clearing.

Mumbling voices grew in my ears.

I peeked through the branches. On the other side of the clearing, Lucky looked back at me with ears perked up. And next to her was Grampa, squatting near a tree with his back to me.

I stepped out into the open, and Grampa turned to look behind him.

"Tomi," another voice said. Charlie. He'd been hidden by the tree.

On the ground between Grampa and Charlie was our *katana*. "Sit," Charlie said, when I got closer.

It was very strange that they were out there in the jungle like that. I sat down and kept my mouth shut. For a few minutes no one spoke, just slapped at mosquitoes and listened to the stream.

"*Shikata ga nai,*" Grampa finally said. "No can help. . . . What is done, is done."

Charlie nodded. "That's right."

What were they talking about?

Grampa picked up the *katana*. He held it in front of him, one hand wrapped in the scarf under the razor-sharp blade and the other on the handle. He was careful not to let the oil from his fingers touch the blade.

With a deep scowl, and very gently, he handed it to me. It almost had a glow to it, of some kind of energy that you felt in your fingers and your chest.

"That belong to your ancestor," he said. "Long time ago. Nobody since then bring disgrace or shame to the name of this family." He paused a moment, watching me, letting his words settle. "My country," he went on. "My *country*, Tomikazu . . . they . . . they . . ."

Grampa turned away, pain carved in his face.

"This island," Charlie said to Grampa, his voice kind. "This territory, Joji-san, this is your country now. You couldn't help what happened. Forget it, already. Wasn't your fault.''

Grampa reached out, and I gave the *katana* back to him. I hoped his hiding place was good, and that he would never bury it like Mama wanted.

"Confonnit," he mumbled. He sounded so lost. Grampa wrapped the *katana* in the scarf and carefully placed it back in the burlap bag that was folded next to him. He tied some brown string around it, then stood and walked off into the trees.

Charlie glanced at me and shook his head.

I pulled Lucky up onto my lap, feeling a sudden loneliness.

Grampa came back without the *katana*. Lucky took off, back over the trail, and the three of us followed in silence. But the feel of the *katana* stayed in my hands.

I would tell Grampa about Sand Island later. If I told him at all.

16

Mari

A couple of days after Christmas, Billy came over with a big smile and his father's binoculars. "Remember these?" he said, holding them up. A leather strap crossed his chest, and the binoculars case rested on his hip, like a canteen. Red, who now followed Billy everywhere, sniffed my foot.

"Sure, your dad's binoculars."

"Not anymore . . . He gave them to me."

"*Gave* them to you?"

"Christmas present."

"You had Christmas?"

"Sure . . . didn't you?"

"Yeah, we had it." That was a lie. I don't know why I said it. We had to forget Christmas, Mama said. We had to save our money. Anyway, we never made a big deal out of it like the *haoles* did.

Lucky and the rest of the pups came out from under the house and swarmed over Red. "Come on," Billy said. "Let's go up in the banyan tree and look at Pearl Harbor."

We walked out to the field, the dogs following, then went into the jungle and climbed to the lookout.

The sky was white with high, thin clouds. It made the ocean silver. The boats at sea were black dots. Billy adjusted the focus on the eyepiece. "You know the *Arizona* burned for three days?"

"Let me see," I said.

Pearl Harbor was busy with tiny men on boats and barges trying to bring the bombed ships back up. Smaller boats passed by each other, leaving crisscrossed V-shaped wakes in the glassy water. You could see jeeps and trucks driving around out on Ford Island in the middle of the harbor.

"Amazing," I whispered. The binoculars brought everything so much closer. "I can't believe your dad gave these to you."

"I know. Me too."

"What did he give Jake?"

"A Colt .45 with a carved ivory grip that Dad got from my grandfather."

"Shee . . ."

"What did *you* get?" Billy asked.

"Uhh . . . a lantern."

"No kidding . . . like a Coleman, or what?"

"Yeah, a Coleman lantern."

"Great."

"Tomi," someone called from the field. Mama.

"What?" I yelled back.

"Where you stay?"

"In the tree . . . wait . . . I'll come down."

Billy put the binoculars in the case and followed me.

"You come home," Mama said when we got to the field. "We going see Sanji family. Downtown." Mama started back to the house.

"You think I could come with you?" Billy whispered.

"Mama . . . can Billy come too?" Billy cringed. Mama turned back and studied him. "Sure . . . you come, Billy."

Billy punched my arm. "Somebody's got to teach you a little tact."

"What's that?"

"Jeese . . . forget it," he said.

· · ·

We took the bus to Sanji's wife's place, which was down near Hotel Street, where the sailors and army guys went for the bars. She lived down an alley as busy and as poor as Kaka'ako. Laundry hung above from one building to the next. The alley was narrow and dirty, the pavement greasy. It turned the bottoms of my bare feet black.

We had to climb to the third floor of a three-story building, up a long flight of creaky wooden steps nailed to the outside. Two doors were at the top.

I looked back down into the alley. Billy stood next to me, keeping back from the railing, which looked like it was about to fall off. People passed below, the tops of their heads moving like round black bugs with feet swinging out in front of them.

Mama knocked on one of the doors.

A lady opened it—Sanji's wife's mother, we soon discovered. Mama spoke to her in Japanese, and offered her the box of eggs she'd brought along. The lady took it. She smiled and stepped back for us to come in. We exchanged bows and nods as we walked by.

The room was small and cramped with furniture— two beds, a table with a few chairs, and an old brown couch. And it smelled bad, like it never got any air. Billy sat down next to me on a wooden chest near the door. It had a thin pillow on it. There was only one window in the place. It looked out to the walkway where we'd come.

Billy whispered in my ear, "What are they talking about?"

"Sanji's wife is out. . . . I think she said they went to the vegetable stand."

"You *think* she said that? Don't you understand them?"

"Good enough . . . I can catch a few words."

"It's so sad," Mama was saying. "My husband loved Sanji like a son." The lady nodded, then stared at the floor with her hands crossed in her lap.

The door opened. A young woman came in. She looked like she could have been a senior at Roosevelt. And behind her, a girl younger than Kimi, carrying a small bunch of bananas.

We all stood up.

Sanji's wife was surprised to see Mama and me, and looked almost speechless to see Billy. Billy glanced down

at the binoculars case, which he held in front of him in
both hands. The little girl hid behind her mother, completely out of view.

Sanji's wife bowed to each of us when her mother
introduced us. "My name is Reiko," she said in English.
"I heard of both of you. . . . Sanji talk about you all the
time . . . talk, talk, talk . . . Billy and Tomi."

Billy gave her a shy grin. Reiko put her hand behind
the little girl, urging her forward. "This is Mari."

Mari smiled, even shier than Billy, then jumped back
behind her mother. Her eyes were dark and clear, and
her hair was short and shiny black.

"She's very beautiful," Billy said. He squatted down
so that his eyes were level with Mari's. He took the binoculars out of the case and started looking through them, at
the wall, at me, at the ceiling.

Mari peeked out from behind her mother. Billy
handed her the binoculars. "Want to take a look?"

"Go ahead," Mari's mother said, gently pushing her
over. Mari put the bananas on the floor and reached out.
She took the binoculars from Billy. They were almost too
heavy for her. "Put your eyes here," Billy said, moving
next to her and helping her hold them up. Mari pointed
the binoculars toward her grandmother. A big smile
came to her face.

Mama and Reiko sat down and talked for a while.
They both dabbed their eyes with hankies as they spoke.
It made me feel awful.

Finally Mama stood up to leave.

"Mari-chan," Reiko said, wiping her eyes. "Give that
back to Billy."

"No, no," Billy said. He slipped the case over his head and handed it to Reiko. "Those are for Mari. . . . I—I want her to have them. . . . When the next full moon comes, take her outside and show her the mountains on it. . . . You can see them pretty good through those things."

Reiko tried to give them back, saying it was too much, but Billy wouldn't take them. "It's okay," he said, not understanding how indebted it would make Reiko feel. She took some money out of her purse and tried to give it to Billy.

"Please," Billy said. "For Mari."

"Take *something*," I whispered to Billy. "It will make her feel better."

He frowned at me, then said to Reiko, "How about a banana?"

She picked up the bananas that Mari had carried in. "Here," she said. "You take."

He nodded, and took them.

Sanji's wife seemed relieved, though I didn't think Billy noticed.

When we were sitting on the bus on the way home, Mama in the seat in front of us, Mama turned around and said, "You nice boy, Billy. . . . You welcome our house anytime."

Billy nodded and said, "Thank you," then turned to look out the window. Wherever Sanji was, I knew he had tears in his eyes for what Billy had done.

17

Sand Island

Thinking about Papa being a prisoner drove me crazy. *Shikata ga nai*—It can't be helped. How could Mama and Grampa just accept it and go on like nothing had happened? Didn't they understand that he was a prisoner of *war*? But he was just a fisherman. He wasn't an enemy to anyone.

When I told Grampa I wanted to go looking for Papa, he got angry and told me to forget it. "You go there, they going shoot you," he said.

"But I'm only a kid."

"They shoot, I tell you," Grampa spit back.

• • •

Dawn. Sky dark and stormlike.

Grampa was already out with his chickens. Heavy gray

clouds moved steadily toward the sea. Today I would tell Grampa I was going to see Rico.

But I would go to find Papa.

I put on a sweatshirt and a pair of shorts and made sure my ID card was in my pocket, then left the house as soon as it was light and the curfew had lifted. Leaves swirled around the yard. A shiver ran through me, as thunder rumbled far off in the mountains, muffled by the clouds.

In less than an hour I'd walked all the way to the harbor, down to where the freighters and passenger ships docked.

What I saw shocked me.

All around the water—everywhere—were barbed wire barricades wound in twisted and jumbled coils from post to post, the wire going all over like it was spun by a lunatic spider. It scared me just to look at it.

To get beyond it to the piers, you had to pass through gates guarded by soldiers.

I waited across the street, trying to figure out what to do next. Sand Island lay across the smooth gray harbor, less than a quarter mile away—a low, flat place covered with scrub brush and a few trees. I could see a white building with a red tile roof out there.

A convoy of army trucks rushed by. Stone-faced men peeked out from under the tarps in back. Behind the trucks, five tanks thundered by, shaking the street. I covered my ears. It was like I was in a nightmare.

The tanks rumbled on, and I crossed the street. How was I going to get over to Sand Island? I didn't even know if it *was* an island, or if there was a spit of land that connected it, or some kind of bridge.

Soon I came to where two army guards stood by an entry station. They had pistols on their belts, and steel helmets and dark arm bands that said MP on them. *They going shoot you.* . . .

I could see their eyes watching me even though they seemed to stare straight ahead. When I came up to them, they got out of that stiff position. I pointed past the barbed wire. "Is this how you get to Sand Island?"

"This area is restricted," one of the men said. He didn't smile or anything.

"I'm looking for my father. He was . . . arrested . . . by mistake."

The guard stared at me a moment, then said, "Better go home, son."

"But he's just a fisherman."

"Beat it," the other guard said.

I peeked past them. Nothing but ugly buildings and shipping boxes and a few trucks. A thick raindrop splattered down on my shoulder. The guards slipped army-green ponchos over their heads.

I headed back, and the rain let loose. Big drops bounced off the pavement. Rivers began to run in the gutters. I looked for someplace to get out of the rain and found an arched concrete bridge. I ducked under it and sat on a ledge, huddling next to the stream that ran out into the harbor.

What a stupid idea . . . I should have listened to Grampa.

The rain came down harder and the sound was deafening. The river started to swell and cloud with mud. I watched it rush by. Across the harbor Sand Island looked so desolate, a ghostly spit of land and the now barely visible red-roofed building.

It was pretty hard to see that far. The rain beat down onto the water so hard, it looked like it was boiling. But I could make out the shoreline across the harbor. No barbed wire over there. I figured they had it strung out on the other side, on the ocean side where the enemy could land.

Barbed wire!

I hadn't even noticed—there was no barbed wire. Not over there, and not here *under* the bridge. Nothing between me and Sand Island. I could swim out there. . . .

But what if someone saw me?

But it was raining, hard. . . . Maybe no one would be out there looking . . . even if they were, the rain was making everything blurry.

I crawled along the ledge under the bridge to the harbor side. No people on the docks and no ships moving around, not even any small boats. It was a long swim, but I was sure I could make it.

Then I remembered the tugboats, like sharks with big magnetic teeth that pulled you under. I'd seen them moving ships up to the pier, huge, sucking propellers churning the ocean white behind them, making giant, ugly whirlpools. If one of those things came by while I was out there, it would chop me into shreds.

Another stupid idea.

But . . .

I took my ID card out and stuck it in a crack on the

ledge, then covered it with my sweatshirt. If I lost that I'd be in more trouble than I wanted to think about.

The water was cool, but not cold. I dropped down into it and let the stream carry me out into the harbor, keeping low so I'd look like something floating, a coconut or some piece of junk in the water.

The rain thundered all around me. I turned and looked back. No one on the bridge. Still no boats, or anyone on the pier. When the force of the stream died out I started swimming . . . breast stroke, keeping low, making as little movement as possible. I accidentally swallowed a mouthful of oily, fuel-smelling water, and gagged. I tried to keep from coughing.

Pull. Easy, steady. Looking back. Watching for boats.

About halfway across the harbor I started to get tired, but at least I could stop worrying about being seen by anyone on shore.

Sand Island . . . were there guards there?

The rain started to let up. It would pass soon.

Move . . . stop thinking about being tired. . . . Keep going, keep pulling.

I didn't realize how tired I really was until I felt the soft touch of watery sand under my feet. I crawled out and stumbled up the small beach to sprawl in some weeds. The rain still fell, but not as hard as before. I curled up into a ball and thought about going back into the water where it was warm. But I stayed hidden in the weeds.

Soon the rain slowed to a drizzle, then stopped. A breeze brought the soft rumble of surf from out on the reef on the other side of Sand Island. It must have been about noon. I rested awhile, then crawled up to the flat land above the beach and into the waist-high weeds.

They going shoot anybody try go there. . . .

Grampa was right. I should just be dutiful. I should be respectful and obey everything he says. *Papa should beat you. . . .*

But I was so close.

I crawled to a thicket of kiawe trees and studied what I could see of the white building. The whole island wasn't that big, maybe a half mile long and a quarter wide. I inched closer, hiding behind the trees.

The weeds broke onto a sandy field riddled with puddles. And beyond that, the prisoner camp.

My chin dug into the sand as I lay flat, straining to see. The camp wasn't much more than a barbed-wire enclosed yard of sand with a bunch of tents set up in neat rows. Beyond that was the white building, and a couple of smaller buildings.

But there was still the open field. How was I going to cross *that?* I could wait until dark and then crawl to the trees on the other side . . . but I had to be home before dark, before curfew. I should just get out of there.

Strange.

No guards. No prisoners. The place seemed deserted. Had I made a mistake? Had I come all this way just to find nothing?

The few trees that stood near the prison fence weren't that far away . . . about as far as from a pitcher's mound to center field. But it felt like three times that much. It was now or never . . . now or never.

I crouched and kept low to the ground. My feet

thumped over the sand, making huge splashing sounds when I hit the puddles. I dove to the ground and rolled into some weeds around three trees. I lay there panting.

In the camp nothing moved. Where *was* everyone?

I counted more than thirty tents sitting in muddy dirt and sand, some shaped like pyramids and some like a sheet staked down over a clothesline. If Papa was there, was his tent near the fence?

The fence, I suddenly realized, was two fences, with about ten feet between them. You'd almost have to shout to talk to someone.

I waited, shivering. Wet shorts and no shirt.

After a while, a long line of men came filing out of one of the smaller buildings. When they got to the tents they broke up and went inside, or just gathered in groups in the yard. A few wandered toward where I was, talking to each other in low voices and looking at the dark sky. They were all Japanese. Still no guards in sight.

I recognized a fisherman I'd seen before . . . a friend of Papa's. He wandered into one of the pyramid tents that was near the fence. Too far away.

In a few minutes he came back out. My heart pounded with each step. Closer . . . closer.

"Pssst," I whispered.

The man stopped and looked around, out into the field, then back toward the tents.

"Over here." I stuck my head up out of the weeds, then quickly ducked back down.

When he saw me he looked around to see if anyone else had seen. "Lie flat!" he commanded, then walked casually over to stand right across from me.

I parted the weeds and peeked through. He stood with his hands in his pockets, looking up at the sky as if checking to see if it was going to rain some more. "Who you? What you doing here?" he said, without looking in my direction.

"Tomi Nakaji," I said in a shouting whisper. "I'm looking for my father, Taro."

He glanced in my direction, then quickly turned away. "No move, boy . . . the guards see you, they going shoot." He started to walk away, then stopped and looked at the sky again. "No even breathe."

He went into a tent and came back with Papa.

Papa looked . . . awful. Unshaven and grimy, far worse than after a month at sea without a bath. He walked slowly, limping. He used a stick for a cane. I wanted to call out to him, to jump up and run over to the fence. I could explain to the guards that they were all wrong, that they had an innocent man. But Grampa's words screamed through me: *shoot you, shoot you, shoot you. . . .*

"Tomi!" Papa whispered, not looking my way, a deep scowl on his face.

"Papa, I—"

"Shhh! No say nothing. . . . You listen to me. . . . Stay in that trees until nighttime, then *go*. . . . You hear me? Go!" Papa looked scared. I felt sick.

He waited there with his friend, both of them scowling at the ground. Papa leaned on his stick, and once peeked over at me. The look on his face was as sad and lonely as I'd ever seen it. His friend said something to him and put his hand on Papa's shoulder.

Finally, Papa whispered, "Tomi . . ."

I lifted my head a little so he could see.

"You very brave . . . but also . . . Tomi, you tell Mama not to worry . . . Tomi . . ."

I wanted to call to him, to tell him I would get him out of there somehow . . . but I kept quiet, like he'd said.

A guard came out into the yard from the white building. Papa's friend urged Papa away from the fence. They separated, and Papa limped to his tent and sat between two mud puddles on a small stool. He sat straight, like Grampa, the stick lying across his lap. He stared out into the wet weeds, away from where I was, his weary eyes sagging.

It was almost unbearable to be so close and not be able to do anything but dig down into the dirt. I had to force myself to stop thinking about it before it made me crazy. I started thinking about food. But the thought of eating made me feel sick. And so did the salty smell of the wet, mushy sand I was lying in.

An hour passed . . . maybe two . . . or three. Papa never stopped guarding my hiding place.

I fell asleep, then woke with a twitch, suddenly remembering where I was. My neck was stiff and hurt when I moved. A blotch of sand clung to one side of my face. I wiped it away and ran my fingers over the grooves it left in my cheek.

I got up on my elbows and peeked over the weeds. Papa was gone. Everyone was gone. It was getting dark. They must have gone back into the building.

Night came down and hid the open field. I crawled

back out of the trees and sprinted across the sand and puddles to the kiawe thicket, then slowed to a fast walk and picked my way through the weeds to the harbor. I must have been crazy to think I could help Papa. *Crazy!*

The water was warm and black.

The city across the harbor hid in a dark silhouette of buildings. An island with no lights. I swam slowly, evenly, trying to pace myself so I wouldn't get too tired. Except for the hum of a small-boat engine somewhere, the harbor was quiet. Off to my left a blue light moved steadily across the water. I waited until the boat passed, hanging in the water with only my hands moving back and forth.

I aimed toward where I thought the bridge was. It seemed like days since I'd hidden under it.

The cool, fresh water rushing out from the river pushed me away from the bridge. I had to swim harder. I turned and worked into it on my back, face to the sky. The clouds had cleared. There were stars by the millions. Seeing them like that, so peaceful, made me feel sad. And lonely.

A *thrumming* . . .

Churning.

Tugboat!

I swirled around, looking for it.

Blue lights bore down on me, growing larger. Sickening gray-white wake.

Boiling wake.

I lunged toward the bridge, my arms so tired they dragged me under. I came up, gasping. The *thrum* grew louder. I could hear the swishing of water shooting out from under the hull, and a voice crackling over the tug's radio. A giant shadow loomed over me.

The sucking grabbed at my legs, dragged me backward.

Sucked me back toward the churning prop.

Nowhere to go but down. I went under, trying to dive to the bottom. Get out of the way.

Down.

The tug thundered above.

Down, down to where the water turned cold.

The tug passed and the sucking stopped.

I waited as long as I could, then clawed my way back up. My lungs felt like they would explode. I broke the surface, gasping for air. My legs and arms could barely hold me up. Swim. Swim to the bridge.

Swim . . .

The ledge was slippery with moss. For a few minutes I just hung on to it, then dragged myself up, the sharp concrete edge digging into my hands and scraping my legs. I lay panting in the dark, my mind dizzy with fear and exhaustion. I fell asleep without knowing it.

Sometime later I was awakened by a kick. A flashlight with a blue-painted lens burned into my eyes. A bayonet poked at my throat.

18

Tough Guys

"**Identify yourself,** and don't move or I'll run this thing through your neck. You have a name, boy? Where's your card?"

An inky black shadow above me. Soldier. MP.

I fumbled around in my pockets, then remembered I'd stuck it in a crack. "It's over there," I said, pointing behind me, afraid to move.

The man moved the bayonet away from my throat. "Get it."

I eased up and rubbed my neck, then inched over to get the card. The MP took it and shined the blue light on it. Quickly, then shut it off.

All black. No moon.

"What are you doing down here?"

"Nothing . . . I was just swimming, that's all."

"At night? Don't you know there's a curfew?"

"I fell asleep." I squinted up at him. Too dark to see his face.

"Get up and come with me."

The soldier backed away. I crawled out after him, shivering. "Don't be stupid, kid . . . this curfew business is dead serious." He paused a moment, the stream quietly lapping past, sounding less swollen, less stirred up. The MP seemed to be thinking about what to do with me. "Count yourself lucky this time," he finally said. "But I'll tell you this—if I ever catch you here again, you're not getting off so easy. . . . You got that?"

"Yessir."

"Where do you live?"

I pointed up toward the mountains.

"How far?"

"Three or four miles, I guess."

"You're a little far from home, aren't you?"

"Yessir."

The soldier studied me, his face faintly visible. My back itched. Salt mixed with boat fuel and river mud. "Come on," he said. "I'll drive you home. . . . I don't want anyone shooting a kid."

I followed him out to the road. The dark blur of an army jeep was parked there, half of it up on the sidewalk. Another MP sat in the driver's seat smoking a cigarette. "What you got there, Mike?"

"Jap frogman."

The soldier in the jeep snickered, then looked me over. The tip of his cigarette glowed, cupped inside his palm.

"We're driving him home."

The other soldier got the jeep going. The man with the rifle nodded for me to get in the back, then he got in the front. We drove away fast. I put my sweatshirt on and gripped the bottom of the backseat, shivering from the cold and trying to keep from rolling out when we sped around the corner and headed on up toward the mountains. The headlights were painted out, so you could barely see the road.

I showed them how to get there. But when we got to my street they wouldn't let me out by the trail that led to my house. Instead they drove up the Wilsons' driveway and swung around in front of the house. The place was dark. Blacked out. I started to climb out, the jeep idling like an old sampan. I prayed Mr. Wilson wouldn't hear it.

"You don't live here, boy," the driver said.

"Next door," I said softly. "My mother works for the people who live in this house. . . . She's their maid. . . ."

The driver smirked and shook his head.

"Go on, get home," the other man said. I jumped out and watched them drive away, the small pinholes of red from the painted-over taillights vanishing as they turned out onto the road. The sound of the engine quickly died away.

Silence. Dark. So dark I couldn't even tell where the trees ended and the sky started.

The Wilsons' front door creaked open and someone stepped out onto the porch. I dropped down. "Who's out there?"

Mr. Wilson.

"You'd better speak up. . . . I've got a gun." The

floorboards creaked as he moved around. I found a stone and tossed it over to the other side of the driveway.

Bam! The sound of Mr. Wilson's .45 shattered the still night air. I took off, running toward the trees.

Bam!

A bullet thwacked through the branches above me.

Bam! Bam!

• • •

Mama stood up when I walked into the kitchen. Kimi, who'd been on her lap, ran over and hugged my legs. Mama smiled at her, and Kimi let go and ran back. Mama put her arm around Kimi and looked back at me, her face hardening. "Where you been?" she demanded.

Grampa drilled me with his eyes, his scowl hard and angry.

Kimi buried her face in Mama's apron and started whimpering. She must have known something was wrong. Grampa told her to hush.

"I—I saw Papa."

Mama let out a gasp and moved over to the table. Slowly she sat down. She turned away from me.

I moved over next to her and kneeled down on one knee. Mama turned back and touched my damp shirt. "You smell like oil. . . . Tell me where you been." I waited a moment before answering, looking at the floor. "Sand Island," I finally said.

No one moved, or even seemed to breathe . . . even Kimi.

"He's okay . . ." I told Mama, speaking quietly, shamefully. "He said to tell you not to worry."

Suddenly Grampa slapped his hands on the table. Kimi jumped and leaned over to bury her head in Mama's shoulder. *"Usotsuki!* You *liar!"* Grampa said, burning me with fiery eyes. "You *no* can get there. . . . You *no can do!"* He stood and leaned toward me, his hands still on the table.

"No, Grampa, I'm not lying," I said, standing up. "I saw him. I swam across the harbor and *saw* him—"

"Tomi, *hush!"* Mama said.

Grampa sat back down. Tears came to Mama's eyes and she quickly wiped them away.

"I know what I did was wrong," I said. "I shouldn't have gone there—"

"Oh, Tomi," Mama said, holding Kimi close, rocking her. The candle on the table flickered in her wet eyes. A wave of dread ran through me. How could I have been so thoughtless? How could I have thought only of myself? "I'm sorry, Mama. . . . I'm sorry."

Mama tried to smile, but couldn't.

Grampa went out the back, banging the door open and letting it slap shut behind him.

I waited a few moments in the deep silence that followed, then went to my room and put some dry clothes on. I lay down on my bed and stared into the darkness.

Mama's shadowy shape appeared in the door.

She put a plate of *musubi* on the bed. "You must be hungry," she said. I took one and almost ate it in one bite.

"We not angry, Tomi. . . . We were afraid . . .

afraid for you. I look in *ojii-chan* eye and I see how he is so worried about Papa, just like me. And then you were gone too.''

Mama sat on the bed next to me and put her hands in her lap. *"Doh sureba iino?* What would we do with Papa gone, and you gone, and Grampa with the stroke? We need you, Tomi. We all need to be together, to help each other.''

I sat up and put my arm around Mama. "I had to know if Papa was . . . was alive. . . . I just had to know, Mama. I promise I won't do anything like that again.'' I leaned my head against her shoulder.

Mama patted my head. *"Daijobo-yo,* Tomikazu. It's all right.''

We sat that way a moment longer, then Mama said, "You very, very brave, but we need you to be brave here.''

After another moment of silence, Mama pushed me back and stood up to leave. "You sleep now.''

I lay back down, my head spinning. Brave? Mama had a husband who had been shot and arrested, a son who didn't think, and who had almost gotten himself killed, an old man who couldn't work anymore, and a five-year-old who was afraid just to go outside. Who was left to keep us going?

And Mama was calling *me* brave.

What a joke.

• • •

On New Year's Day Billy showed up in my yard with his baseball mitt. It was sunny and clear. No clouds, no wind. "Come on," he said. "Get your stuff. We have a game to play with the Kaka'ako Boys. . . . Remember?"

"Are you kidding? *Baseball? . . . Now?*"

"If we ever needed baseball, it's right now. . . . Come on, let's go."

I didn't know if he was joking, or what. All I could think about was Sand Island and Papa's sagging eyes. I guess I needed a joke, but who could laugh.

I shook my head and started up the steps to go get my glove. I stopped, then turned back. "Come inside," I said.

Billy hesitated. Then he shrugged and said, "Sure," and followed me in.

I stood back so he could see my room. "This is it."

Billy looked around at my bed, at Grampa's mat and the orange crates. "I like the shelves," he said.

"Yeah."

Billy smiled and said, "Let's go." What had I been so worried about all those years?

I knew Mama didn't want me to go anywhere, especially after Sand Island. But she trusted me when I told her I'd never try anything like that again. "You come home before nighttime" was all she said.

For once, some things seemed to be returning to something like normal—though anyone could tell the old familiar way would never come back. But right now I didn't want to think about that. "What about Rico and the other guys?" I asked.

"I called Mose, and he talked to some of the others. And Rico went down to talk to the Kaka'ako Boys. He said it took some doing to get those guys together. Some of them had to get jobs and can't play anymore after this game . . . because . . . you know . . . their fathers got arrested, and things like that."

Arrested.

First we walked over to Mose's house, where he and Rico were waiting with their mitts and two bats. "Let's go," Rico said as we walked up to them. He tossed one of the bats to Billy. We picked up Rodney Lasko, Randy Chock, Maxey Matos, and Tough Boy. Then finally, Kaleo Kepo'o, our fastest base runner.

"Hey, Tomi," Mose said as we all walked down toward Kaka'ako. "You found your daddy yet?"

The question startled me.

"He's at Sand Island, like the police said."

"Shee, sorry, man. But at least you know where he is, yeah?"

"I went to see him."

Mose stopped and looked at me. "How? You no can go out there unless you're army."

"I swam."

"You *swam*? Through the harbor?"

"It was raining. Nobody saw me. But I saw my father, and he saw me. We couldn't talk, but I saw him."

Everyone was listening now.

Billy looked shocked. "You could've got killed," he said.

I nodded and looked down at my feet.

"Criminy, Tomi," Rico said. "How come you did that?"

I shrugged.

Mose shook his head. "You got guts, man."

Rico mumbled his agreement.

As we walked down to Kaka'ako I tried to stop thinking about Sand Island. Think about baseball, I kept telling myself. But it seemed crazy to play baseball when less than a mile away Papa was limping around behind barbed wire fences.

But being with my friends like that felt good.

We tried to look mean, so that no one would bother us. Plenty of eyes rolled our way. Rico carried a bat across his shoulders with his arms hanging over the ends of it, making sure everyone saw his gangster scar.

When we got to South Street, I reminded Rico that Herbie Okubo's brother had told us to avoid those Coral Street guys. "What?" he said. "You swam to Sand Island and almost got shot, and you want to hide from those punks? Come on, man."

"We came for baseball," I said, "not to fight."

"Wait," Mose said. "I got an idea."

We followed Mose to the corner just before Coral Street. "Okay," he said. "Tomi, you and *haole* boy go down the street like last time." I looked at him like he was nuts.

"No worry, just go."

"Come on, don't fool around," I said. "Those guys—"

"No worry, I tell you. Billy, give me that bat. You won't need it."

Hesitantly, Billy gave Mose the bat, and the two of us turned the corner and headed down the street. And there were the punks. Five of them.

"Heyyy," the ugly big guy said when he spotted us

coming. "Look who's back, the frickin' *haole* and the *haole*-Japanee. . . . Hey, where's your frens this time?" I glanced back to see what Mose was up to.

"Nobody back there," the big guy said. They surrounded us. "How come you so stupit?"

I started to say something . . . actually, I almost started to beg . . . but then they glanced up the street behind me. I looked back.

Mose, Rico, and the Rats, their faces cold as ice, came strutting down with the two baseball bats. "Hey," Rico said. "You punks bothering my frens again?"

The big guy's eyes darted around.

Tough Boy poked his finger into the big guy's chest. "Move."

And he did.

Tough Boy pushed through, and the rest of us followed, giving them all deadly stink eye.

The Kaka'ako Boys were waiting for us, lined up like the black and gold Mick Sluggers they hoped to be, tossing balls back and forth and taking practice swings. And there was the Butcher, practicing his wild pitches. Sometimes Hamamoto, the catcher, had to stand up or fall to the side to get them. I cringed when I thought of one of those speedballs coming at me, busting my head, maybe, or my knuckles.

"Look at that babooze," Rico said, pointing his chin toward the Butcher. "One good crack from him and you in the grave, man."

We strolled out toward the diamond, still puffing up like Grampa's movie samurais. I wondered what the

Kaka'ako Boys thought when they saw us, them so real-time-baseball-looking, and us looking like . . . Rats.

Ichiro Fujita, their leader, and the brains, smiled and came over to talk.

He nodded to Rico. "You ready?"

Rico leaned on the end of the bat. "Give us five minutes to warm up, then get ready to lose."

Ichiro's teeth gleamed in the sun. "You remember the Butcher, don't you?" He turned and glanced over at the pitcher's mound.

"I seen him already," Rico said. "He throw pretty fast, but no can aim, yeah?"

Ichiro smiled bigger. "Better keep your eyes open."

Rico tried to smirk, but he couldn't, because he liked Ichiro. At least, he respected him. "No worry about us. . . . Worry about how you going face your friends after you lose."

Ichiro ignored him and looked at me. "How'zit, Tomi? You folks okay?"

I nodded. "Except they arrested my father."

Ichiro shook his head and looked at the ground. "Sorry, yeah."

"Yeah. How's about your folks?"

"Okay. My father works for Tuna Packers, and they don't call that dangerous, I guess. But some of the other guys on the team not so lucky. They gotta get jobs to support the family. How 'bout you?"

"I guess I need a job too," I said.

The thought hit me like a brick.

Ichiro went back to his team grim-faced.

"He's okay, that guy," Rico said. "I almost sorry we going make him look bad."

The Kaka'ako Boys were up first.

I squatted down behind home plate and sent a fastball sign to Billy. The batter dug his toes into the dirt and took a couple of slow practice swings.

As I waited for Billy to move into his pitch I noticed the five Coral Street punks, with seven new guys, settling down on the grass. Three of them had·baseball bats of their own. But they weren't there to play.

19

The Kaka'ako Boys

With two outs in the top of the third, Herbie Okubo got a hit off Billy. Herbie's ballahead older brother showed up to watch. He sat under a tree on the third-base side.

Billy was pitching like a champ . . . and so was the Butcher. He was right on target. All you saw coming at you was a white blur that popped into Hamamoto's mitt before you could even think about it.

Herbie's lucky hit off Billy should have been the third out. But Herbie got just the right amount of fly on it, and Tough Boy couldn't get out to it before it hit the ground.

Tough Boy threw it to second, hard.

Herbie stopped at first.

Right after that, Ichiro Fujita came up to bat. I gave Billy the two-fingered curveball sign.

For once I didn't feel like razzing Ichiro at the plate. "Billy's pretty hot" is all I said.

"Maybe, maybe not," he said back, keeping his eye on Billy.

Billy's curve was perfect, just like at diamond grass.

Ichiro swung and fouled it up.

I ran back and caught it, and the inning was over.

Ichiro slammed the bat into the ground.

Billy scowled as he walked in from the mound.

"That was a perfect curveball," I said.

"They got a hit."

"Don't worry about it. They didn't cash it in."

"Naw, I guess not."

The game went on with nothing happening until the top of the eighth, when the Butcher came to bat and guessed the fastball pitch that I had signaled to Billy.

Tock!

Right on the sweet spot. The ball sailed out past right field and into the street for a homer. The whole team came out to greet the Butcher when he came strutting across home plate. Billy was so mad he took the next three batters out, bam, bam, bam. All clean strikeouts.

We came up in the bottom of the eighth.

Rodney went down on a three-pitch strikeout. The Butcher looked pretty smug out there, and the Kaka'ako Boys were rubbing it in. "You play like sissies," someone yelled. "Come on, give us a challenge."

Tough Boy came up to bat. He spread his feet apart and dug in, tapping the old cracked home plate with the tip of the bat.

The Butcher's first pitch went the way we had all been fearing . . . wild.

Of all the guys the Butcher could have beaned, it was Tough Boy that he cracked on the arm. Tough Boy fell to the ground and rolled around, writhing in pain. We all stood to see if he was okay. Red with anger, he scrambled up and started walking toward the Butcher. All the Kaka'ako Boys came running in from the field, and we all ran out. Billy grabbed Tough Boy. "Forget it," he said.

Tough Boy shrugged him off and kept on walking toward the Butcher.

"Hey, sorry, yeah," the Butcher said, his hands spread apart. "It slipped."

It was the first time I'd heard him speak. His voice was unnaturally high, kind of like a girl's. Spooky, almost. I think it surprised Tough Boy too.

Tough Boy came right up to the Butcher's face, only the Butcher's face was a mile higher. Tough Boy glared at the Butcher, then said, "That's okay, man . . . just don't do it again."

The Butcher rolled into a wide, stupid-looking grin. "If I do that again, you can come punch me . . . free, I won't stop you."

Tough Boy nodded, and went to first for getting hit. I wanted to shake his hand.

On the next pitch Billy got a hit and made it to first. Tough Boy ran all the way to third. Nobody out. The Kaka'ako Boys got pretty quiet. Randy Chock was next to bat, then Kaleo, then Rico.

Randy popped a fly ball to center field for the first

out. But after the catch, Tough Boy raced in and crossed home plate standing up. Billy stayed at first.

We went crazy cheering.

Tied. One to one.

The Butcher's first pitch to Kaleo was right in near his hands. It had come so close, Kaleo stood back for the next one. Way back. He ended up striking out, worrying that he'd get hit. That Butcher was smart.

Two outs.

The Butcher's first pitch to Rico was inside too. Rico flinched, but didn't back off. He smiled and dug in.

Rico connected on the next pitch and the ball flew all the way out to the Coral Street punks. It hit the ground and bounced right up to them. One of them picked it up and tossed it in to the outfielder, who sent it back to the infield. Billy ran all the way home, but Rico had to stop at third.

Two to one . . . but it should have been *three* to one.

"*Cheat, cheat!*" we all yelled, standing and waving our fists. The Kaka'ako Boys ignored us.

I was up next, but my hands were shaking, I was so mad.

"Come on," Rico yelled at Ichiro, walking halfway out to first base. "That was a cheat!"

"What?"

"Those punks threw the ball in."

"Who?"

Rico glared at Ichiro, then came back and told me to hit it all the way to China.

I popped the first pitch up and the inning was over.

Me and Rico and Billy ran up to Ichiro Fujita. "Rico's hit should have been a homer," Billy said.

"I never saw nothing," Ichiro said. "You like be a crybaby, or what?"

"That was a cheat," Billy said. "Those guys out there threw Rico's hit back in."

Ichiro shook his head. "Never saw that."

A couple of other Kaka'ako players came over. "Come on, let's play," one said.

Ichiro kept his eyes on Billy. "You like play that inning over? We can do that. . . . We can play the whole frickin' inning over, if you want. But I never saw nothing."

I was beginning to believe him. But it still didn't make it right.

Billy and Ichiro shot poison arrows back and forth, their eyes squinting down. Only baseball could get Billy that hot.

"No," Billy finally said. "Even if you cheat we can beat you."

Ichiro smiled. "You ain't gonna win."

So now we were leading, two to one. Three outs to victory. But the Butcher got another homer off Billy, which made Billy so mad you couldn't even talk to him. We would have won already if the Coral Street punks hadn't thrown that ball in.

When we came up to bat for the last time, it was Mose, Maxey, and Billy.

Mose went down on a foul tip that ended up in Hamamoto's glove. The Butcher's first pitch to Maxey was so wild it went *behind* Maxey.

The Butcher smiled. "Sorry," he said in his high, squeaky voice.

"Shhhh," Maxey said, then spit and waited for the next pitch. High. Hamamoto had to stand up to get it. Dust flew off his glove when it hit.

"Easy, Maxey, easy," Rico said. "You got 'um. . . . he's rattled."

"Easy for you to say," Maxey called back. "How would *you* like to stand here when this guy is rattled?"

"You can do it," Rico said.

The Butcher didn't look too happy.

Maxey waited.

Thwack!

A fastball. Maxey let it pass, probably hoping it would be out of the strike zone. But it was dead on. Strike one. Maxey tried to argue, but not very hard. And we kept quiet, because it clearly *was* a strike. After all, when you play without an ump, you have to be at least a little honest about it.

Maxey swung at the next one and missed. Strike two.

The Butcher was smiling again, and making dumb "watch this" faces to Ichiro at first base. Ichiro punched his mitt and waited, his glove out in front of him, ready for anything.

But the Butcher sent two more wild shots across the plate. Maxey walked to first.

Billy came up and squinted out at the Butcher, ready.

But Billy didn't get a hit—he *got* hit.

Right on the foot.

The Butcher was losing his touch. Ichiro Fujita and Hamamoto went out to calm him down while Billy hobbled to first and Maxey jogged to second. "Okay, okay, okay," Rico yelled, clapping his hands. "Let's go, let's go, let's *go!*"

Rodney Lasko, our shortstop, came up next. The Butcher stared at him a long time. It made Rodney nervous, so he stepped out of the batter's box, waited a minute, then came back and got into his stance.

That Butcher took Rodney out with three straight ace pitches—one, two, three. They were so fast Rodney was swinging long after the ball had already hit Hamamoto's glove.

Rodney threw the bat away and walked back to the rest of us.

Two outs.

Maxey on second and Billy on first.

I felt kind of sorry for Tough Boy, who was up next. It was our last chance.

The Butcher studied Tough Boy while Maxey and Billy danced around a few feet from their bases, raising dust and heckling the Butcher. Out and back, out and back, like yo-yos.

The Butcher's first pitch was a rising fastball that Hamamoto had to reach up for. Tough Boy held his ground and didn't fall for it. Ball one.

"Let's go, Gayle," Hamamoto said. "Slow down . . . you can take him."

Tough Boy looked back at Hamamoto. We all heard it.

Gayle?

"Who that?" Tough Boy asked Hamamoto. "Who?"

"Gayle."

"The pitcher, who else?"

"His name is *Gayle?*"

"Yeah, so what?"

Tough Boy grinned. "That's one girl's name."

"So? Tell *him* that." Hamamoto punched his glove.

The Butcher stared in at Hamamoto's sign. He nodded, then straightened up. He peeked over at Billy, who was a third of the way to second. The Butcher jumped and Billy dove back to first on his belly. The Butcher—Gayle—laughed. It sounded like a giggle. He giggled so much he started to cough.

"Hey, whale," Tough Boy yelled. "Send me a sweet one, yeah?"

The Butcher's smile disappeared. "Whatchoo said?"

"I said send me one sweet one."

"No, what you went call me?"

"Gayle . . . that's your name, right?"

Whap!

The Butcher's wild pitch missed Tough Boy's head by inches. Tough Boy hit the dirt, then got up and brushed himself off. "Ball two," he said, smiling.

The Butcher's next pitch was slow, and Tough Boy was guessing fast. He was finished swinging by the time the ball crossed the plate.

"Strike one," Hamamoto said.

The Butcher carved into Tough Boy with razor eyes. Billy and Maxey tried to distract him with their base dancing, but the Butcher wasn't going for it.

On the next pitch Tough Boy got his sweet one.

Tock!

I loved that sound, just like on the radio. That ball was gone, gone, gone . . . all the way to the street. Maxey came home, Billy came home, and Tough Boy didn't even bother to run to second. The game was over.

We went crazy.

The Kaka'ako Boys came in from the field with sour faces, saying nothing, just going off and packing up their stuff. We jogged over, the cheat forgotten, and said things like "Good game," and "You guys one tough team, man," but all we got back were a few "Yeahs."

We congratulated ourselves and gathered up our gloves and bats and headed off toward Lucy Street.

"Hey," someone yelled. "Hey, you sissies."

The punks, with their bats and tight fists, surrounded us.

The big guy came in and shoved Kaleo. Rico slammed into him and everyone jumped in. Somebody's fist landed on the side of my head. It stung, and I could feel my scalp getting hot.

The fighting stopped as quickly as it had started. The punks backed off.

Then I saw why . . . the Kaka'ako Boys.

"Whatchoo trying to prove?" Ichiro said to the big guy. "These boys my frens, no mess with them."

"What, you like me slam you too?" the big guy said. He was almost twice Ichiro's size.

"Just try it," Ichiro said. The Butcher came up behind him, a little bit of murder in his eyes.

The big guy spit. "Frickin' baseball sissies . . . frickin' *tillies*."

The gang backed off and slowly walked away. They

looked back every now and then, just to let us know that they weren't done with us. There would be another time.

"They won't bother you anymore today," Ichiro said. The Kaka'ako Boys muttered their agreement, then they all started away in a pack.

"Eh, Fujita," Rico said. "We owe you one."

"Nah, that one was for the cheat."

"You punk," Rico said, smiling.

"You the punk," Ichiro said.

Criminy, I was going to miss those guys.

20

Lucky

Billy was right about how if we ever needed a game of baseball, that was the time. I slept like a lead sinker for three nights in a row.

But in the middle of the fourth night, I woke up in a sweat, breathing hard. Grampa struck a match and lit the candle that he kept by his mat. The room glowed with low, jittery yellow light. My sheets were damp and twisted.

Grampa leaned on his elbow, and squinted over at me. "You dreaming."

A nightmare . . . Parts of it still lurked in my mind. I sat up and stared down at the shape that was Grampa. He was kind of fuzzy. At first I didn't think it was him. I saw Papa instead—the dream—Papa lined up with Sanji and a bunch of other fishermen, all of them on their knees. There was a firing squad, the men getting ready to shoot. I couldn't remember if they shot or what, but I could remember Papa smiling . . . smiling at me . . . *This is a good place, Tomikazu,* he was telling me . . . *Take the boat, stay . . . have a couple of kids.*

"Boy," Grampa said.

I moved my feet off the bed so they touched the floor, and tried to shake those awful thoughts out of my head. "I'm okay, *ojii-chan.* . . . It was just a dream . . . like you said."

"Uhnnn," Grampa mumbled, lying back down. He pinched the candle flame out with his thumb and middle finger.

I got up and crept through the dark house to the porch and sat on the top step. Lucky came stretching out from under the house and trotted up the stairs. She sat next to me and yawned. Her breath was sharp. A couple of her puppies wandered out. I could barely see them, it was so dark.

Something scurried through the bushes and Lucky's ears went straight up. "Mongoose," I whispered. "Or a rat."

This is a good place. . . .

Think of the game, think of baseball. . . . Papa is all right, stop worrying. And Sanji . . . Mari . . . no, no, no . . . don't think about that. Think about baseball . . . baseball. . . .

I sat there with Lucky for about a half hour, then went back to bed. The dream was almost gone, but I still felt uneasy.

• • •

Grampa had to wake me the next morning. "Go look the porch," he said, nudging me. Seven o'clock. I'd slept late.

I bolted up. Out on the porch someone had left a five-gallon gasoline can. "What's this?" I asked Grampa.

"Kerosene."

"Where'd it come from?"

"Look the name on the side."

MATSON NAVIGATION COMPANY, in scratched and fading white letters. Five gallons of kerosene. For our stove. For our lantern. That stuff was as good as gold, and almost impossible to get.

Mr. Davis . . .

"Mama!" I called.

But Mama already knew about it. "Go get fifteen eggs, Tomi. Take 'um to Billy's house. Then go find a can. We going take some of this kerosene to Sanji family."

I took twenty-three eggs to the Davises. Every one I could find.

• • •

That afternoon, Billy came over with Red, and a ball and a bat. He found me at the chicken coops with Grampa and Kimi. Lucky and her pups ran off with Red.

We'd collected fourteen more eggs. Mama wanted me to take them down to the store and sell them, or trade them. She'd asked me to help Grampa because he was going to kill himself if he didn't relax a little. "He worry too much," Mama had said. "Bombye he going get more stroke, Tomi. . . . *You* the man now. . . . You do that work.''

''Come, *ojii-chan,* ''I said now. ''Rest for a while. Come with me and Billy.'' I could do his work later.

''For what?''

''For nothing. You don't need a reason to take a break.''

''No got time for that.''

''Aw, come on, Grampa . . . you got the time. I'll do this chicken work for you later. How's about it?''

Grampa eyed me. ''You clean this chicken coops?''

''Yeah.''

''You take this eggs, sell 'um?''

''Sure, come on.''

He thought for a moment, making me wait, like he was doing me a big favor. He was so *irritating,* sometimes. ''You pick those weeds from by—''

''Grampa!''

Grampa gave in and came along, bringing Kimi. He acted as if it didn't matter to him if she came or not. But he didn't fool anyone. He knew that Kimi was still scared from the planes and explosions.

The two of them sat near the trees in the shade while Billy pitched his perfect curveballs. Those moments at diamond grass kept me from going crazy—thinking about what was going to happen to Papa, and what was going to happen to us. But nobody knew anything at all.

''We need a batter,'' Billy said, raising his eyebrows and tipping his head toward Grampa.

''Grampa, come bat,'' I called.

Grampa threw his head back and laughed and laughed and laughed. I looked at Billy.

Grampa slapped his knee and kept on laughing. Then Kimi started laughing. Billy gave me a what's-so-funny look. Grampa only laughed at the movies.

"Come on, Grampa . . . come hit the ball. . . ."

Grampa stopped laughing when he saw that we were serious. He scowled at me, then glanced at Kimi's big eyes, and her smile. "Confonnit," he mumbled, and creaked himself up.

Kimi stood up, too, and started jumping up and down.

Grampa broke into a grin and rubbed Kimi's head, then walked over to the bat. I took off my glove and showed him how to hold it and how to swing it. "Just look at the ball, Grampa . . . then crack 'um when it comes by."

Grampa shoved me aside.

I put my glove back on and squatted down, punching my mitt. "Grampa DiMaggio up to bat," I shouted to Billy. "Send him a good one."

Billy made a big show of giving the pitch a royal windup—stepping back, then kicking his leg extra high. He sent a slow, easy ball across the plate, one Kimi could've hit.

Grampa swung before the ball was even close. He lost his balance and staggered. He growled to himself and came back to the plate. I tossed the ball back to Billy.

"Way to go, way to go," I said to Billy. Then I whispered, "Just keep your eye on the ball, Grampa."

Billy wound up and sent another one that practically

floated across. This time Grampa smacked it . . . about five feet, anyway. It hit the ground and rolled through the grass to Billy.

Grampa started jumping up and down like a crazy man. "Eh, busta, good, nah? Wa-ha-ha-ha-ha-haaaaaa . . . good, nah? Wa-ha-ha-hahahahaha."

We all started laughing. You couldn't help it when you saw that sour old man in such a good mood. It was like the olden days again, me and Billy at the movies, rolling in our seats and watching Grampa laughing at Laurel and Hardy.

Grampa dropped the bat, slapped the dust off his hands, and strutted like a rooster back over to Kimi. He was okay, Grampa. . . . For the first time in my life I could see a little bit of Papa in him. And, I could hardly believe, a little bit of *Rico*.

I heard dogs yapping somewhere, and growling. Lucky came racing out into the field with all four puppies chasing her, trying to catch something she was dragging by her teeth . . . something white. . . .

"*Jeeze!* They dug up the *flag!*"

Me and Billy and even Grampa ran over to catch her. "Lucky," I called. "Stop! Lucky!" But she swerved away. "Come back here, you mutt."

"Go that way," Billy yelled, and we circled around the pack of frenzied dogs from opposite directions. Lucky saw what we were doing and headed farther out into the open, the white-and-red flag flopping over the grass behind her.

"Hurry," I yelled. "Someone will see it!"

Grampa came out and closed off Lucky's run from his

side while Billy and me worked around the ends. But it wasn't any of us who outfoxed her. Red broke away from the stumbling pack trailing the flag and took a shortcut.

"Get her, Red boy," Billy called.

And he did . . . caught up and latched on to the flag, slowing Lucky down enough for me and Billy to tackle her. Red tried to get the flag away for himself, but Billy pulled it out of his teeth and held it up over his head.

"Lucky, you crazy dog!" I said. "You want to get us *arrested*?" She and Red kept jumping up and trying to bite the flag.

Grampa took a long, sorrowful glance at his flag from across the field.

"We'll take care of it," I said.

Grampa turned away and acted as if it didn't matter to him what we did with it. He took Kimi's hand and headed home.

When he was out of sight, Billy grinned and said, "They were having a pretty good time, weren't they?"

"Yeah, having a good time giving me a heart attack . . . Come on, we got to bury that thing under a pile of *stones*."

Which is exactly what we did.

• • •

At sunrise the following morning, Grampa rode away on his bicycle, the rusty old fenders rattling down the bumpy path into the trees. I yawned, standing next to Mama at the front door.

"Where's he going?" I asked.

"Downtown," Mama said. "Last night up Charlie house, *ojii-chan* heard they going send Sand Island men to mainland."

"*Main*land? Why?"

"*Shira-nai* . . . I don't know . . . *ojii-chan* going try ask somebody . . . *wakara-nai* . . ."

Mama moved away from the door slowly, like she was getting old. She had so much to worry about. And what could I do? Nothing. But I had to do something. The mainland was a place somewhere far across the sea. California, Arizona, New York. How could we ever go there? How could Papa ever come back here?

Kimi and I ate a silent breakfast, with Mama sitting and staring out the window. When we were done, I asked Kimi if she wanted to go collect the eggs from Grampa's chickens. She nodded, and we got the bucket from the back steps.

We brought back seventeen eggs—five for us and twelve to trade at the grocery store. "After store," Mama said, "you go see Charlie. Try find out when school start again."

School.

I'd almost forgotten about it. I missed seeing Mose and Rico, and Mr. Ramos. I missed riding in the car with Billy and Mr. Davis. I wondered if we'd still do that. "Tomi," Mama said. "What you daydreaming about? Somebody knocking."

I stuck my head out of the kitchen. Mrs. Wilson was peeking through the screen. "It's Mrs. Wilson," I whispered to Mama.

Mama froze. Mrs. Wilson had never been over to our house before.

She rapped again, long and hard.

Mama hurried to take her apron off. She patted her hair.

"Mrs. Wilson," Mama said. "Come inside, please." She opened the door.

"No, thank you . . . I . . . can only stay a minute."

Mrs. Wilson glanced around our small front room. She looked nice, like she was dressed for church. I was very relieved that the emperor was buried under the house.

"Is something wrong?" Mama asked.

"No . . . It's just that . . . well, Keet . . . He was supposed to come down to tell you that I . . . that we . . . would like you to come back to work . . . starting today. . . ."

Mama didn't say anything.

"You have a very good friend in the Davis family," Mrs. Wilson suddenly went on. "John and . . . Mr. and Mrs. Davis came over last night to speak to Mr. Wilson and me in your behalf. We, of course, have been worried, but they assured us that your family is completely loyal to the United States." She studied Mama before going on. "So . . . well . . . we've decided to have you return to work."

Mama thought for a long moment, then said, "I come fifteen minutes."

Mrs. Wilson nodded. "Good." She rubbed her hands together like she was washing. "Yes . . . fifteen minutes, then."

She turned and started down the steps. The pups jumped like grasshoppers around Mrs. Wilson's legs as she picked her way through them and hurried off into the trees.

• • •

After the sun went down and the first stars poked into the sky, Grampa came home. He walked the bike back up the path. "They gone already," Grampa told Mama without looking at her. "Mainland."

"Where on the mainland?" I asked.

"Jus' mainland . . . on one boat."

Silently Mama watched Grampa walk the bike around the side of the house. Her face showed nothing. No sadness. No anger. Papa might as well have gone to the moon.

I sat on the steps and studied my dusty feet. "What are we going to do now, Mama?"

"We going be strong, that's what. . . . We going wait and we going be strong."

I can't do this, Mama, I wanted to say.

I can't, I can't, I can't. . . .

21

The Katana

Two days later Billy and I walked down to see Mose and Rico. We fooled around at Rico's house, and had a good time being lazy bums out of school. Rico bragged about how he was making progress with Tough Boy's sister, Tina. But who believed him? Tina was a tenth-grader, and way too classy for a guy like Rico. He just didn't know it.

At about five o'clock, we started back up the valley. The streets were busy with people trying to get home before curfew—except up by our place, where it was as quiet as a coffin. A lot of people who lived around there had evacuated to the mainland on the first boat they could get a ride on.

When we walked by the Wilsons' I glanced up. There was a black car parked in the driveway. It was parked only halfway up to the house. And the Wilsons' car was gone. So what was this one doing there?

We passed by and went into the trees, following the path to my house. Someone was yelling . . . *Mama!*

I started to run.

"No . . ." I heard her say. "Let him go."

I ran faster, sprinting up the trail. "No, no," Mama was begging.

I burst out of the trees and ran into a man. Billy bumped into me from behind.

"Watch it!" the man said. There were *two* of them, both huge. And hanging between them, looking like some old jacket on a hanger, was Grampa. Each man had a hand under one of his arms. Mama was trying to pull Grampa back. The first man knocked her hand away.

"*Grampa,*" I said. "What's happening?"

Grampa spoke quickly. "*Katana,* Tomikazu . . ."

"*Hey!* Speak English," the smaller man said. They pushed past, dragging Grampa between them. I followed, keeping off to the side. Mama went back to Kimi, who was screaming on the porch.

"Tomikazu . . . *katana o mamore!*" Grampa said. The men turned and headed toward the Wilsons' house.

"*Nakaji no namae o mamore!*"

One man covered Grampa's mouth with his hand. They kicked weeds and bushes aside and cut through toward the black car. Rufus charged down, barking. I ran after them, and tried to pull the man's hand off Grampa's mouth. He shoved me away, and I fell into the weeds. "*Grampa!*"

Billy ran over and helped me up.

Rufus barked and snarled and nipped at the men all the way to the car. Grampa stumbled along between them, glancing back at me. One man opened the back door and pushed him in, then slid over next to him. The other man got into the front and started the car. Rufus bit at the tires as they backed down the driveway. The car bounced out onto the road, slid to a stop, then sped away.

The Wilsons' house loomed over me. *They* did this, I thought. Keet and Mr. Wilson. *They* called those men to come take Grampa. An explosion burst inside me, hot and wild. I ran across the yard, jumping the low hedge along the driveway, leaping up the steps to the front door.

Bam! Bam! Bam! Bam! Bam! "Come out of there!" I screamed. *Bam! Bam! Bam! "Come out of there!"*

Billy ran up and grabbed me, pulled me away. "Don't, Tomi. . . . Hurry, let's get out of here."

"They did this to Grampa!"

"You don't know that. . . . Come on, let's go before you get in trouble."

Billy grabbed my shirt and pulled me off the porch and back into the trees. I wanted to burn their ugly house down. "Come out of there," I yelled. "Come out!"

"Let it go," Billy said.

The farther away I got from that place, the more the monster inside started to scare me. I'd *never* felt like that before. Billy put his arm on my shoulder and urged me toward my house. "We'll find where they took your grampa. . . . Let it go, Tomi, let it go."

I shrugged Billy's arm off, and instantly wished I hadn't. But I couldn't help it.

Mama was sitting on the steps hugging Kimi, who was still sobbing. I thought Mama would be crying too. But she wasn't. She was angry.

"What happened?" I managed to say. Breathing hard. Legs shaking. The swelling in my throat strong.

"They just come and take him," Mama said. "No tell why. No tell nothing."

"But who were they?"

"FBI."

I had to sit down. My head was spinning. Dizzy. First Papa, now Grampa. "*Why*, Mama . . . ? Why now?"

Mama didn't answer. Just sat there pressing Kimi close. Her hand fanned the back of Kimi's head.

"What are we going to *do*, Mama?"

"We going do just like always," she said. Still hugging Kimi, Mama got up and carried her into the house.

Billy and I sat on the steps. I tried to think. Everything had happened so fast.

"Damn," Billy whispered.

"Why . . . ? Why Grampa?" I wasn't even sure if it *was* the Wilsons. They weren't even home.

"What did your grampa say?"

I thought for a moment, trying to calm down and pull it back. "He said to save the *katana* . . . the sword."

"What sword?" Billy asked.

"A samurai sword that he had. It's . . . sacred to us. And he said to protect the family name, and not to disgrace it."

We sat there thinking while the sun burned out, Billy

with his elbows on his knees, and me bent forward with my arms buried in my stomach. Lucky dozed under the steps and thumped against the boards whenever she scratched.

Finally, Billy got up to go home. "I'm really sorry," he said, looking back at me.

"Yeah . . . I'm sorry too. . . . I was kind of nuts."

"I would've been too."

•   •   •

That night Mama sat alone in the darkness of the front room—an unmoving shape on the couch, with the emperor's bare wall looming over her.

"Mama?" I said.

She didn't answer, just sat there staring at nothing.

I waited a moment, then started to leave.

"When I first came to this islands was more worse than this," Mama finally said.

Silence.

I waited, standing next to her in the dark.

"My husband-to-be was dead from gambling. I only knew three women, and they went with their new husbands. I only had one small box of clothes."

She paused again. I remembered the story Grampa had told me about Mama the picture bride, and how she had arrived to no one, to nothing. How scared she must have been.

"I came this islands to make new life, and with your good papa, that's what I did. I could survive then, and we can survive now."

"Yes, Mama."

"You must find work, Tomi, make a little money to help. Kimi can do Grampa's chickens, get the eggs and sell them. I will work for Mrs. Wilson, like always."

Mama thought for a second, then went on. "She good woman, Tomi. She was just afraid before. Did you know she gave us that meat we had last week?"

That surprised me. I thought Mama just got lucky at the store. "Mrs. Wilson?"

"Yes. Was her."

Kimi's soft crying drifted in from Mama's bedroom.

"Go to Kimi, Tomi," Mama said. "No worry about me; I just need to think."

Kimi's wet tears dripped onto my hand. "It's okay, Kimi, it's okay," I whispered. "Go to sleep."

She let out a small cry, a small sob. "I want *ojii-chan* . . ."

I hugged her, suddenly feeling like more than her big brother. "He's a strong old man . . . no one can hurt him. . . . Wherever they took him, Kimi, no one can hurt him."

She finally fell asleep on my lap. I moved her over on Mama's futon and covered her with a sheet.

I went to my own room, holding my hands out in front of me as I crept through the blacked-out house. You could only see shapes, dark against darker. Grampa's mat was a gray rectangle on the floor. I sat on my bed staring down at it for a long time.

I got that trembling in my ears, that trembling that came from fear or sadness or hate or what, I didn't know.

Why Grampa? *Why?*

• • •

Dawn.

Barely. The sky was purple-black.

Mama was already clinking plates in the kitchen.

I dressed quickly and slipped out of the house, inching the screen door open just enough to squeeze past. The air was warm, but the grass was wet and cold under my feet. I prayed Charlie knew where Grampa had hidden the *katana*. It had to be somewhere near where I'd found them that day, sitting in the jungle.

I took the trail Grampa's own feet had dug out of the weeds from years of going to listen to the police. Grampa. *Arrested*. Where was he? What was he doing now? Would they send him to the mainland too?

I rapped on Charlie's door and peeked through the screen. "Charlie," I called.

No answer.

I walked around back to the garden, and found him squatting on his heels, pulling weeds. He saw me coming and stood, and wiped his hands on his pants.

"They arrested Grampa," I said.

Charlie gaped at me. "Joji-san?"

"The FBI . . . they took him away. . . ."

Charlie just stared, his mouth half open, his eyes vacant. Then he shook his head, and said, "Tst . . . chee . . . why they did that?" He frowned at the dirt.

"He had that flag," I said. "Maybe that's why . . . I don't know."

"Sure he had it . . . Why not? That was his country."

"But . . . they attacked us, and—"

"He was *ashamed* of that. They wrong about him . . . they wrong."

"Grampa wanted me to get the *katana*," I said. "Where did he hide it?"

"Inside one log that was rotten in the middle."

"Can you show me?"

"What?"

"The sword . . . show me where it is."

Charlie put his hand on my shoulder, still grimacing. "They wrong," he said again. He led me out of the garden and into the jungle.

. . .

The *katana* was wrapped in the burlap bag and hidden inside a soft, rotting log, just like Charlie had said. I took the bag off, and the scarf, and pulled the *katana* out, careful not to touch the blade with my fingers. The steel gleamed and flashed in the sunlight that fell through the trees. "That thing was very important to him," Charlie said. "His history . . . *your* history, Tomi."

I felt the weight, the quality.

Ancestors. Honor. Respect. It was all just an old man's talk. Something I'd always listened to with only half of one ear, if even that. But now Grampa counted on me to save it all, save the *katana*. Not *my katana* . . . but the *family katana*. It belonged to no one, and to everyone

. . . past, present, and future. Thinking about it made me nervous.

"Put oil on 'um, so no rust," Charlie said. "Then hide that thing someplace safe . . . and don't take it out until this war is over. . . . Some people scared when they see that kind of things."

I wrapped the *katana* back up and tied the string around it. Charlie patted my shoulder and left me alone in the jungle.

This is a good place, Tomi. . . .

I tried to believe that Papa and Grampa were there with me—in the brilliant sunlight that streamed through the trees, in the warm earth and the sea that surrounded the island—not in some camp on the mainland. Not in some jail downtown.

I hiked deeper into the jungle and came to a small clearing.

I wanted to look at the *katana* again.

Grampa had kept the steel polished. I could see my face in it. I thrust it out in front of me, trying to hold it in one hand. It was as heavy as an ax. I tried to swing it around, but could only do it with two hands. I didn't know how those samurai guys lifted these things, except that they usually had two *katanas,* long and short, one in each hand, and maybe they balanced each other somehow.

"Haaa!" I said, swinging the *katana,* slicing the air.

"Hold it right there, fish boy."

I jumped and swung around, still holding the *katana* with both hands.

Keet Wilson came out of the trees, his .22 raised to his

cheek. The rifle was pointed at my head. "I *knew* you were in on it," he said.

"In on what?"

"You know what I'm talking about. You and that old man and the Jap flag." He took a step closer, then stopped, squinting down the barrel with one open eye.

"I wasn't in on any—"

Bam!

A bullet whizzed over my shoulder and thwacked through the trees. "Shuddup!" Keet said, and I froze. "Drop that thing."

Slowly I bent down and put the *katana* in the dirt.

"Back away from it."

I did, shaking.

Keet lowered the .22, still keeping the rifle aimed at me. "Move."

I backed away to the edge of the clearing.

"Where'd you get that thing?"

"It's my grampa's . . . it's been in our family for hundreds of years."

"Shhh," Keet scoffed. "He probably got it at a carnival." Staring straight into my eyes, he lowered the rifle more, aimed it at the *katana*.

Bam!

The *katana* bounced. Dirt exploded in a puff of dust. Keet cocked the rifle and sent another bullet into the chamber. A brass shell flipped to the ground. When the dust cleared, I could see a small nick in the handle. My fists were as tight as hammers.

I stepped toward the *katana* and reached down to

pick it up. "Touch that and the next bullet goes in your hand."

I looked up at him. Our eyes locked. Slowly I kept reaching, my eyes on Keet.

"I *mean* it, punk," Keet said. "I'll shoot."

Bam! The dirt near my hand puffed and fell back.

I picked up the *katana.*

Keet grinned at me. "You little pecker."

I found the *furoshiki* scarf and burlap bag, and put the *katana* away, then slowly backed into the jungle. Bushes closed around me. Keet burst out laughing. "Hey, my dad's gonna go nuts when he hears about that sword."

I stopped and moved a low branch aside so I could see him, so he could see me. "You're not going to tell him anything."

"Oh, yeah? Why not?"

"You're not that stupid."

"What does *that* mean?"

"It means if you tell *anyone* about this sword and someone takes it away from me because of what you said, I'm going to make you pay for it . . . and not in money."

Keet laughed again. "Yeah? You and whose army, shrimp?"

I stepped back out into the clearing, into the sunlight. "Me and *this* army," I said.

"What? I don't see no army."

I tapped my chest with the tip of my finger. "This one."

"You?" he said, then laughed harder.

Finally he stopped and stared back at me. He cocked the rifle—hard—brass shell flying out. Then he turned and walked back into the jungle.

I thought I would pass out.

22

Not Far From Pearl Harbor

Near the end of January, we got a postcard from Papa. It was addressed in care of the Wilsons. Mama brought it home after work.

"Tomi," she called, "Kimi-chan."

She was almost too excited to speak. She said Mrs. Wilson had read it to her several times already, but she wanted us to hear for ourselves. She hurried us into the kitchen, and made us sit at the table. "Read it," she said, handing me the card.

I quickly read the whole thing to myself. The date said it had been sent weeks ago. There was no return address, and the place where it says where it was mailed from in the postmark was blacked out by a censor.

"Read," Mama commanded.

To my family,
A soldier is writing this for me. To write in Japanese is not allowed. Do not worry about me. The soldier is a good man. I am treated well, and many of my friends are here with me. This is all a mistake that will be corrected soon. Tell Grampa to watch the boat, and tell Tomi to find a job until I come home. Tell Kimi to help Mama. Tell Mama not to worry. Tell Tomi to feed the pigeons, and tell him to help Sanji's family.
Nakaji Taro

"He doesn't even know about his pigeons," I said.

For a long time the three of us sat silently at the table, each of us touching and studying the card with no return address that Papa had sent. By now he must know, I thought. He must know that the army isn't even *trying* to straighten out the mistake.

Honor yourself, Tomi, and you honor us all. . . .

Yes, Papa, yes. But where is the honor now?

Mama got up and covered the window with the blackout blanket, then lit the lamp and went over to the shelves to find something to cook. Our small supply of food was growing smaller. Kimi slid off her chair and went over to help her, just like Papa had said.

Mama smiled at her. "How old you now, Kimi-chan?"

"Five," Kimi said.

"Five? That much? You almost grown up, already." Mama shook her head. "Well, if you that old, then it's time to teach you how to cook rice."

Kimi beamed and peeked over at me to see if I'd heard.

• • •

Early one morning Billy rapped on our door. He'd been running. It was hot out, and small beads of sweat glistened on his forehead. "Come on, lazy bones, get your stuff . . . school's on again."

It took a moment to sink in. School had been out for almost two months.

"*School,*" Billy said. "Remember? Books, homework, Mr. Uncle Ramos? Come on, Dad's waiting."

"Mama!" I called, and she poked her head out of the kitchen. "We got school again. . . ."

Mama gawked at Billy and me a moment, then said, "Go change those clothes. . . . Kimi can come work with me. . . . Go." She shooed me off with her hands, and the faintest smile.

When we got to Billy's house Mr. Davis was waiting by his car in a suit, leaning against the front fender with his arms crossed. He stood when we walked up to him. "Nice to see you again, Tomi." He put his hand on my shoulder. His shirt was blinding white in the morning sun, and his shaving lotion smelled good. "I did a little research," he said. "I found out where they sent your father. . . ."

I nearly stopped breathing. "Where?" I whispered.

"Crystal City, Texas."

Crystal . . . City . . . Texas. "And Grampa?"

"Don't know that yet, but I'll keep trying." He

paused, then added, "They'll be okay, Tomi. . . . I know that's not much . . . but . . ." He shook his head.

"When will they come back?"

"That I can't answer . . . I don't think anyone can right now."

"But . . . they didn't do anything. . . ."

"I know they didn't, son."

Billy stood next to his father, watching me. It was funny how much they looked and acted like each other. Both tall, both concerned.

"I want you to know one thing," Mr. Davis said. "If you or your mother ever need anything . . . *anything* . . . you come to us, okay?"

I nodded.

"Good." Mr. Davis smiled and tapped the side of my arm. "Let's go. We don't want you and Billy to be late on your first day back."

* * *

Roosevelt was almost like a ghost town. Some of the teachers and half the seniors had quit, and signed up with the army. And not only that, the navy had put barbed wire all around the school grounds because they had been using the buildings as barracks.

Rico thought it looked pretty good that way. "Look like they went fight here," he said after we'd all met out front like we used to. "But I don't see no blood spots."

"Shee, Rico," Mose said. "How can you say that? Guys died, you know . . . on those boats. It's not right to say things like that. . . . Come on, man."

Rico kind of frowned, like he knew Mose was right.

Billy changed the mood. "Hey, how do you like your gas masks?"

"Shhhh," Rico said. "Make you look like a monster."

"That's for sure," I said.

Each of us had one slung over his shoulder in an army-colored canvas bag. You had to carry it everywhere you went, even to the bathroom. When you put it on you looked like an ant in a microscope.

"You heard about how they need workers for the pineapple fields?" Rico said. "You can work there on Saturdays and still go to school."

That's what I could do. Yeah. I could sell eggs after school, work in the fields on weekends, and get a job in the summer. I'd give all the money to Mama. "I want to do that," I said.

Mose and Rico said they did too. I didn't know if Billy would, or if he even could if he wanted to. He didn't say anything. I just hoped he wouldn't have to go back to the mainland. Of all of us Rats, he was the only one who even had a chance to get out.

It was good to be back, sitting on the grass outside the school, even if there was barbed wire all over the place. But I couldn't help thinking about the battleships in Pearl Harbor, and of all the men who had died there. What about their families? And what about all those innocent people like Papa and Grampa who'd gotten caught up? What about my friends and the boys in Kaka'ako who'd had someone taken away from them—fathers and uncles and grandfathers? A lot had happened . . . a lot of bad things. Thinking about it made me sad. For Mama. For Sanji's wife, and Mari. For everyone.

"Mr. Uncle Ramos was at our house last night," Rico said. "He's going to enlist. This summer, after school ends."

"Really?" I said. That shocked me.

"Going join the navy," Rico added. " 'The army can rot,' he said. But he also said that if the army needed him he would think about it."

Mose looked away and kept to himself. How could you imagine Mr. Ramos in the navy shooting guns? Or getting shot.

The bell rang and we strolled into the building, our gas mask bags bouncing on our hips. "Look," Rico said, opening his bag. Inside with the gas mask were three Hershey bars, the last of his supply. You didn't see those things in the store anymore. "Good place to hide 'um, yeah?"

Mose just shook his head, still frowning.

Mr. Ramos sat on his desk rubbing his busted knuckle and waiting for everyone to settle down, which didn't take long because we were all curious to hear what he was going to say.

"Welcome back . . . Is everyone here?"

"Tosh Yamada isn't," someone said. "He had to take over at his father's store."

"And Myra," a girl added. "She had to get a job too."

Mr. Ramos's smile disappeared. He shook his head. "Eighth grade . . . tst . . . too young to have to do that. But the world isn't the same today as it was the last time we were here." He moved his eyes from face to face. We all stared back at him.

Silence.

"Tomi, how's your family?"

"Okay," I said, and looked down at my hands. I didn't want to tell the whole world that my father and grandfather had been arrested. When Mr. Ramos didn't say anything, I peeked up.

"Mose, Rico," Mr. Ramos finally said. He sounded a little more cheerful. "How you boys doing today?"

"Pretty good," Rico answered.

"Yeah," Mose added, sliding down in his chair.

Mr. Ramos turned back to the rest of the class. "What happened here could happen anywhere," he said. "People have been making war on other people for centuries."

He paused. "Does anyone have any idea why this happened? Why the Japanese attacked Pearl Harbor?"

No one raised a hand.

Mr. Ramos let the silence eat at us. Rico finally broke it. "They wanted to sink our ships."

"That's true, Rico. But there's a bigger reason than that. What do you think it might be?"

Rico got into his thinking scowl, then said, "Because they don't like us?"

Mr. Ramos smiled at that, and the rest of us loosened up a little. My own mood changed with almost every word he said.

"I guess it's true that the government of Japan doesn't like us at the moment," Mr. Ramos said. "But the real reason—the reason at the bottom of all the wars in the history of human life—is power. It's like a drug. Some men can't get enough of it. They want your power and my power and everyone else's power. They want it all for themselves. Adolf Hitler, who started this thing, is one of those men."

I didn't understand. What power?

Mr. Ramos looked us over a moment, then asked Rico, "If you wanted to get into someone else's class because you thought I was a lousy teacher . . . could you?"

"I guess so," Rico said, shrugging.

"You could. You and your mom and dad could talk to the principal and get him to put you in Mrs. Collet's class, or Mrs. Elbert's class. That's power. Power to make a decision about yourself, then make a change if you want to. If you wanted to read a book about Tarzan instead of reading your science book, could you?"

Rico smirked. "Sure . . . I do it all the time."

Everyone laughed.

"That's power too," Mr. Ramos said passionately, reaching out his open hand and closing it into a fist. "There are all kinds of small things that we never think about that give us a little power . . . and all those little powers add up to a pretty good amount."

"Yeah," Mose added. "Like we could do whatever we want after school, even forget about our homework, if we wanted to."

"That's right, Mose," Mr. Ramos said. "And if you wanted, you could even do *more* homework, so you could go to college, and get a job that you like, one that you choose for yourself. But think about this: What would it feel like if you *couldn't* do anything you wanted after school? What if you were forced to keep your mouth shut and work in the cannery from the minute you got out of here until ten o'clock at night? Even if you didn't want to?"

"I'd hate that."

"So would I," said Mr. Ramos. "Not because of the work, but because it wasn't my *choice* to do that work. So . . . what is power?"

There was another long period of silence.

"Freedom to make our own choices," Billy finally said.

"Freedom to make our own choices," Mr. Ramos repeated slowly. "Our *own* choices . . . Did you ever consider how valuable that is? Did you ever think that there are people in this world who *don't* have that freedom? Who have to do what they're told by people who don't care about their individual lives?"

He looked us over, letting it sink in. "Well, there are millions of people like that . . . *millions* who don't have the freedoms you have, the power over their own lives that you have. How do you think it would feel to be one of them?"

We shuffled around and murmured among ourselves that it would be really lousy.

"None of us would like it," Mr. Ramos said. "And that's one of the reasons the human race has wars: people fighting back. People fighting to keep the right to make their own choices, to keep the right to live a free life. Japan thought they could bring us to our knees by bombing our ships, and then they would come in and take our power. But they were wrong. We're not about to give anything up so easily." Mr. Ramos's fist reminded me of Rico's cousin Esther. It took some power to save her.

Mr. Ramos slid off the desk. He looked tired, and kind of dreamy. "We're going to go on in this class just as we'd planned. Boys not much older than you are out there fighting for all of us, and we're going to help them. We're going to show them that we have the spirit to go on despite all that we've been forced to suffer. And don't any of you worry," he said. "We're going to be okay. All of us."

I hoped that included Papa and Grampa.

"Okay," Mr. Ramos said, clapping his hands together. "We're a little bit off schedule, but we can catch up. As I recall, I've had personal interviews with each of you about your projects . . . except for two students."

Mose groaned quietly and slid even farther down in his chair.

"You two know who you are," Mr. Ramos went on. "But in case you forgot, I'll give you a hint . . . it was something about a volcano."

As soon as school let out, Mose was all over Rico. "You stupit . . . was your idea, so *you* gonna make 'um, not me."

We walked down to the bus stop with the two of them banging each other with their gas mask bags. But I was thinking about Sanji . . . and Grampa and Papa . . . and about the *Taiyo Maru*.

"You guys go ahead," I said. "I want to walk."

"Whatchoo mean, walk?" Mose said. "Too far, man."

"I want to go down by the canal and see if I can find my father's boat."

"I thought they sunk it," Billy said.

"Yeah, but the canal isn't that deep . . . maybe I could see part of it."

Rico shrugged. "Okay, walk then . . . but we going with you."

Mose said, "Like Mr. Uncle Ramos told us, we got the power to do whatever we like after school, yeah?"

Rico grinned. "Yeah, we got the power. . . . We're the Rats, aren't we?"

You couldn't help but love those guys. The Rats . . .

But it was sad, like being in my room without Grampa. How could anything be the same? We didn't even have the Kaka'ako Boys to play anymore. "Right now," I said, "I feel more like a kicked dog than a Rat."

"Kicked dog?" Rico said, hanging his arm around my neck. "We ugly, but we don't kick no dogs."

• • •

The canal, not far from Pearl Harbor, was a dirty, rusty brown. But it was easy to find where they sunk the boats. There were a bunch of them, maybe ten. The bow of one stuck out of the water, and a couple of masts came up in other places. Charlie said he'd heard on the radio that they were sunk by a storm, not by the army. But that wasn't what Grampa had heard. Anyway, it didn't really matter. The army dragged them into the canal, and now the *Taiyo Maru* was sitting on a bed of mud.

We found Papa's boat right away, close to shore where

the canal was pretty shallow. The roof of the deckhouse was resting an inch or so under the surface of the water. You could see bullet holes in it.

The four of us sat down on the grass and stared at the jumble of sunken boats, with Papa's right in front of us. The sun lit up the submerged deck. In the back, you could read *Taiyo Maru*. Everything looked rusty and old from the water.

"What's that on the deck? Bullet holes?" Rico asked.

"Yeah," Mose said. "Chee . . ."

"Sanji . . . the guy that was killed," I said. "He was only nineteen."

"Yeah," Billy said in a sad voice. "And he was a good guy too."

We all sat in silence. Who could talk? I kept seeing Papa waving at the P-40s before they shot him. Waving, waving . . .

I shook my head, trying to get those awful thoughts out. I threw a small stone and watched it wobble down to the deck of the *Taiyo Maru*.

"They must have chopped a hole in the bottom," Mose said. "The top part's in pretty good shape . . . except for those holes."

"Maybe we could get some big guys and some ropes," Rico said. "We could drag it up."

Mose frowned. "Are you kidding? What you need is a crane. . . . Water is heavy, you know. And that boat's *full* of water."

"Even if you could get it out, and even if you could fix the bottom, it wouldn't matter," Billy said. "Nobody's going to let you use it."

"That's what I don't get," Mose said. "Why they sunk these boats, anyway?"

"Because the army, or the navy, or somebody, figured they were taking fuel out to Japanese submarines," Billy said. "Or if they weren't, they could if they wanted to."

"But Tomi's father wouldn't do that," Rico said.

Billy shook his head. "Doesn't matter. The army can't tell what's in somebody's mind, so they just went after everybody."

"Stupit, man," Rico said.

"Yeah, but right now they don't have time to think about it. All they know is the Japanese creamed us, and they don't want it to happen again."

I considered what Billy had said. "Yeah, I know that, but my father's as loyal to this place as *you* are . . . so is Grampa. . . . It's *wrong*, what they did."

It got pretty quiet for a moment.

Billy frowned and looked out over the canal. "Wrong, but . . . criminy, I don't know. . . . Listen, all of us here believe exactly what you believe . . . that it was a *bad* mistake. But look at it this way . . . at least they're alive. . . . Look what happened to Sanji."

Mose and Rico nodded silently.

• • •

After a while we got up and started back toward the mountains. I tried to remember the *Taiyo Maru* as I'd always known it—old, fishy-smelling, white, cutting the ocean like a knife, its sharp bow high and proud. Papa steering with his knee, gulping in the ocean air. I saw

Billy and Sanji, sitting on the fish box with Billy's binoculars. Looking at the moon. Quiet voices and moonlight crossing black water to the boat. To see Papa's sampan rotting in the dirty canal made me feel sick to my stomach.

Papa . . . Grampa . . . don't worry. I can watch out for Mama and Kimi. I can do it. I will do it.

"Hey, wait a minute," Rico said. "I forgot." He stopped and opened up his gas mask case. He pulled out one of the Hershey bars. "Here, we can split it." Rico tried to break it up, but he couldn't because the thing was so melted it stuck to the paper. "Aw, shee," he mumbled. "I guess we gotta lick it off."

When we got to the street that headed away from the canal, we passed two men working on a car. One glanced up when we passed by. "Hey, Buddhahead—you got a lot of nerve coming out in the open after what you people did."

I stopped in my tracks and gaped at him. He glared back.

"Whatchoo know about anything?" Rico said.

The man stood up, wiped his hands on a rag, then threw the rag in Rico's face. Rico jumped back when the rag hit him. "You frickin' grease bag," Rico said. He clenched his fists and started toward the man.

Mose and Billy got in front of him and pushed him back. "Come on, Rico," Mose said. "Let's get out of here."

"You better watch your mouth," Rico shouted at the man. He held up his fist and shook it. "Next time you going end up with this down your throat."

"Wait a minute, Rico," I said.

That surprised Rico, and for the moment he kept quiet.

"You got it wrong, mister," I said. "I was born here. I live here, just like you do. And I'm an American."

"Beat it, Jap," he said.

Be above it, Tomi. . . .

"American," I said again.

He narrowed his eyes but didn't say anything more. I eased away feeling . . . strange . . . very strange. Almost peaceful. Spooky, feeling peaceful when somebody hates you. But still, even though I felt calm inside, my hands were shaking.

Rico walked away backward, Mose and Billy pushing him, and me following. "I like bust his stupit face," Rico said.

Billy put his hand on Rico's shoulder and turned him around.

"I could flatten that bag of futs with one hand," Rico spit.

"Forget it already," Billy said.

Pretty soon we forgot about that guy and were all shoving and surging from one side of the sidewalk to the other.

The Rats.

It sounded good a couple of months ago, but now we were better than that. But the name fit us like a soft old catcher's mitt.

"What you so serious about?" Billy asked.

"Just . . . thinking," I said.

This is a good place, Tomi. . . .

• • •

When we were almost to where Mose and Rico lived, it started to rain, not big drops, but a soft mistlike rain that drifted down from the mountains.

"*Kahiko o ke akua,*" Billy said.

"What that means?" Rico asked.

"I don't know, but Charlie always says that when it rains. He says rain is a blessing. The heavens are trying to let you know you're okay . . . that they approve of you. That's how the old Hawaiians felt about it, anyway."

"Makes sense."

"Hey," Billy said. "How could I forget to tell you guys this? You know what? Next year I can stay at Roosevelt."

"*What?*" I said.

"I didn't even have to fight for it. Last night Dad took me out in the backyard and let me pitch to him. He said, *'You still want to stay with your friends at Roosevelt?'* I said, *'Yeah, sure I do,'* and you know what he said? He said, *'Then that's what I want, son. I want what you want.'*"

"No kidding," Mose said.

Billy shook his head. "*'I want what you want.'* . . . Can you believe it?"

Me, Mose, and Rico let out a loud whoop. Mose and I punched each other's arms, then started in on Billy's. "That's great, *haole* boy," Mose said.

"Hey, that's my pitching arm."

"Come on, you stupits," Rico said, pushing us away. "That arm's headed for the majors."

"How come you don't go to McKinley?" I asked Billy.

"They got a first-rate team. You could get recognized and maybe get a scholarship."

"Yeah, well, I could do that at Punahou too."

"But Roosevelt doesn't even have a team."

Billy grinned and flicked his eyebrows. "Says who?"

"Yeah," I whispered.

Mose punched his hand. "Yeah, says who?"

"Hey, maybe *we* could be the team," Rico added.

"Welcome to the party, Rico," Mose said, shaking his head.

Mose laughed and put his arm around Billy's neck. Billy put his arm around mine and I hooked mine around Rico's. We started up the street in the rain, stumbling from side to side like four drunk army guys.

We were the Rats, confonnit. Nothing would ever change that.

• • •

Early one Sunday morning a few weeks later, Reiko and Mari showed up at our house with a small bucket half full of fat brown crawfish they'd caught in the stream. Reiko's eyes swelled with tears when she thanked Mama again and again for the kerosene, which they'd been using very sparingly. Mama's eyes got watery, too, and she invited Reiko and Mari to stay for lunch and help us eat the crawfish.

I took Mari and Kimi out to the chickens so Kimi could show Mari how to collect eggs, which was now Kimi's most important job, along with cooking rice and sweeping the house.

As I followed Mari and Kimi with their two cans of eggs back down from the chicken coops, I decided that tonight I would take out the *katana* and carefully rub away any spots of rust I found on the blade. Then I would run the oilcloth over it and let Kimi hold it. I would tell her where it came from, and why we needed to protect it and keep it clean, and what it stood for. I would tell her that Papa and Grampa would be so proud of her when they came home and found out that she knew all about why we still had it after all these years.

When they came home.

We would all be there and we would cry from being so happy when Papa and Grampa finally walked back through our squeaky screen door with Lucky leaping at their feet. Papa would smile and hug Mama and Kimi and me. And maybe even Grampa would too.

Then later I would bring out the *katana*, all shiny and oiled and looking like the day it was forged, and I would hand it to Papa. He would glance at Mama, then at me, and I would look firm, like Grampa.

Papa would hand the *katana* to Grampa, and Grampa would take it and gently turn the blade in the light. Then he would look deep into my eyes.

And nod once.

Epilogue

In 1945, after World War II ended, all Hawaii Japanese who had been interned or relocated were released and allowed to return to their homes in the islands. Unfortunately, many of them had no homes to return to, all their earthly possessions having been taken from them. In the 1980s, forty years after the fact, the United States government finally acknowledged that it had made a mistake, and agreed to pay each of the survivors $20,000 in reparations.

Many had already died.

Not one Hawaii Japanese man or woman was ever convicted of espionage or sabotage against the United States of America. In fact thousands of Hawaii Japanese gave their lives fighting for the United States. In 1943, the mainly Japanese-American 442nd Regimental Combat Team of the United States Army was formed, and became one of the army's most decorated units of World War II. The 442nd earned more than 18,000 individual medals of valor, including a Medal of Honor, 52 Distinguished Service Crosses, 8 Presidential Unit Citations, 588 Silver Stars, and more than 9,000 Purple Hearts.

Graham Salisbury is a descendant of the Thurston and Andrews families, some of the first missionaries to arrive in the Hawaiian Islands. He grew up on Oahu and on Hawaii. He graduated from California State University, and received the MFA degree from Vermont College of Norwich University.

He has worked as the skipper of a glass-bottomed boat, as a deckhand on a deep-sea fishing boat, as a musician and member of the rock band Millenium, and also as an elementary school teacher. Today he manages an historic office building in Portland, Oregon, where he lives with his family.

His first novel, *Blue Skin of the Sea,* won the Bank Street Child Study Association Children's Book Award, the Norma Klein/PEN Award, the Judy Lopez Award, the Oregon Book Award, and was selected as a Best Book for Young Adults by the American Library Association, a *Parents' Choice* Award book, a Best Book of the Year by *School Library Journal,* and a National Council of Teachers of English Teachers' Choice.